GW00992426

The
EVE
STONE

The EVE STONE

JAYNE THOMAS

DAISA & CO
Est. 2003

The Eve Stone published in Great Britain in 2020

Written by Jayne Thomas

Copyright © Jayne Thomas 2020

A CIP catalogue record for this book is available from the British Library.

Paperback ISBN 978-1-9162251-4-5

Book cover design by: Daisa & Co Publishing

Book typeset by:
DAISA & CO PUBLISHING
Barton upon Humber
North Lincolnshire
United Kingdom
DN18 5JR
www.daisapublishing.com

Printed in England

Daisa & Co Publishing is committed to a sustainable future for our business, our readers and our planet. This book is made from paper certified by the Forestry Stewardship Council (FSC), an organisation dedicated to promoting responsible management of forest resources.

All that is gold does not glitter,
Not all those who wander are lost;
The old that is strong does not wither,
Deep roots are not reached by the frost.

From the ashes, a fire shall be woken,
A light from the shadows shall spring;
Renewed shall be blade that was broken,
The crownless again shall be king.

J.R.R. TOLKIEN

CONTENTS

PROLOGUE
THE BAD NEWS

I picked up the discarded prophecy and it felt like lead in my hands, "Mother, read it to me please, I need to know what has happened. Could it be a mistake?"

Her face was white and her eyes lifeless.

"It's no mistake, the Flame Gods don't lie."

'Your son is missing among the dead, if not dead now, he will be soon as betrayal of blood has come to pass. Only one of his blood can find him alive or dead, cast off or casting for a catch.'

I didn't understand what it meant but I got the gist, that Gallam was lost, perhaps lying dead on a burning battlefield somewhere.

The two of us have never really been close. My older brother had tolerated me, and I had disappointed him. I wasn't a brother; maybe someone to help him fight the abuse? I think he suffered more than myself, as he always seemed to have a sense of wanting to belong, which I have never had. He was led by the feeling of what is right rather than what he wanted to do.

For me, even at the age of 14, it was more important to be free than to follow the laws and traditions. I suppose we were and are both very different.

When he finally gained his surname of 'Krim' he wanted to celebrate; celebrate gaining the name or celebrate surviving the Skims and their bullying tactics, I wasn't sure. Then he was rewarded with the right to fight in a war that seemed miles away and had little or no impact on our lives. He was happy to go, but it was more about independence and adventure and making someone proud, rather than a true allegiance to the Harridans.

The official letter arrived at the cottage later that day, delivered by a Harridan messenger. All those that worked for the Harridans had to wear blinders which capped their eyes and made them look forward only. This was how the Harridans kept tight control; there were so many rituals and secrets that should not be seen. Only the Harridans could know things, those that worked for them should not see or indeed be tempted by what was available. He did not speak or indeed acknowledge me as he handed over the letter. I only caught a glimpse of his goblin-like face, with a large hooked nose and beady black eyes. As he walked away, I could see that his hands and feet were larger in comparison with his limbs and he looked awkward and uncomfortable.

I read the message which was concise:

GALLAM KRIM MISSING. PRESUMED DEAD.

I left it in my mother's hand and ran to my castle, seeking escape. Whilst leaning on the old battlement wall I could feel the comforting coldness of the stones against my body. I'm sure I saw Heligan glide past, her flowing purple robes of the Harridan gave the impression of floating and a flash of her auburn hair gave her away.

I looked over the wall and she seemed to disappear into the trees. I feebly called her name; knowing she wouldn't hear, I decided to follow her instead. I couldn't see her as the thickets of the forest became entangled and the deep green seemed to soak up all the light. But then I caught a glimpse of her red hair and knew I was on the right track. She seemed to be standing still and mumbling indistinct words. I thought perhaps she was practising for a ritual but there was a deeper voice replying to hers, like a harmony.

I was careful as I crept nearer, my feet barely touched the exposed tree roots and my fingers deftly steadied myself on the trunks. There she was, a vision of purple and red. I wondered to myself if my love for her went deeper than that of a friend. I found her so fascinating, so beautiful, but I think I wanted to be her rather than possess her.

A knot tightened in my stomach whenever I saw her, and a rush of excitement ran over me like pins and needles. Mesmerised by the waves of her hair, I suddenly noticed a hand knotted in the curls that seemed to pull her head sideways; her face was hidden by a mop of blonde hair. She was kissing Ethan!

A fight started within me, I wanted to shout out to her, tell her this was suicide. This would mean the end of her Harridan career. At the same time, I also wanted to stay silent and just watch the closeness and enjoy the warmth that was radiating from them. I leaned on the trunk and tried to calm my racing heart.

I scurried back to the castle, careful not to make any noise, and raced into the protection of its walls. I don't know if I was more disappointed that Heligan was with Ethan or that she was risking everything for him. If the Harridans found out it would mean a terrible punishment and she would lose her status as an Earth Sister and all that came with it.

'Why would she put herself at risk like that?' I already knew the answer. It was love and it was then that I realised she loved him more than she loved me; I felt the hot sting of tears in my eyes. I crouched down into a ball against the old wall, hugged myself and cried myself dry.

When I was done sobbing, I wiped my face with my sleeve and cleared my eyes. 'Grow up and stop feeling sorry for yourself.' I thought.

A glint of green caught my eye as I looked at the floor. On closer inspection, I could see a pebble lying between two broken pieces of grey stone. It was beautiful, a green smoothness mottled with intense rough seams of a radiating yellow.

I held it tight in my fist and its warmth emanated through my skin, giving me comfort and a feeling of renewed energy. The stone's energy seemed to sing to me, knowing exactly what I needed.

I knew then that I would make it my talisman. I promised myself that every time I touched this stone, I would feel grateful for everything I had in that moment and forget about everything I had lost or was about to lose.

I placed the stone in my pocket and made my way home...

CHAPTER ONE
RAYKAL AND HELIGAN

Have you ever thought about touching the walls of an ancient castle? It seems cold, hard, and soulless at first but then the warmth of centuries, of people lost and their untold stories seep through the stone, into your fingers making them tremor, and you come alive, tingling with voices of the past.

Tarnade Castle was my sacred space during these days of war and discontent. Its cracked and ruined shell seemed to offer some protection, the moss ridden walls dulled the noises from the outside world and I found comfort in the embrace of the once impenetrable walls. My broken castle was nestled within Burn Ash Forest; I knew little of its history but welcomed the snippets of legend and folklore whispered by the Harridans.

The Harridans were our rulers, Earth Mothers that congregated in the forest to worship the earth. Times were rotten they said, the safe world that we had come to know would soon perish. They reiterated this repeatedly, as they danced and called on spirits to save us and show us the way.

I often watched them dance by firelight, hidden behind a low wall, softened by heather. I longed to join in their mystic rites, but I was shunned for being a child with no father and labelled an 'Unnamed'.

Tarnade was naturally a beautiful place, but then it was all I knew; made up of wooded groves, and stream laced fields leading out to vast green plains. The sun often shone gently in the summer and in the winter the wind whipped up and howled restlessly through the trees.

Nature in Tarnade was beautiful but its people were a different matter altogether. The small collections of thatched huts were splattered in crevasses of woodland, and farms were stashed in crisscross fields. Communities were disconnected fragments, often fuelled by suspicion and fear of rule breaking, so much so, that human connections suffered.

There was only one shared place and that was the central Marketplace which opened one day a week. It suited the ruling Harridans to keep people apart; the splintered people hung on their every word and law, believing the Harridans to be the saviours of the land. As a result, it was a fractured, disjointed society that was pincered by harsh rules and regulations and the people were judgemental, critical and suspicious of anything outside of Harridan rules.

The Harridans were revered as saviours, leading us from disorder and chaos. They resided in the Fortress, the only fortified building in the land. Although they slept there and held court there, their real home was Burn Ash Forest. It was here they carried out their secret rites and rituals.

On the edge of the forest, I waited to talk to Heligan. She was only two years older than me and often shared secrets that weren't supposed to be told. She was impetuous, still caught up in the newness and exclusiveness of being part of the Harridan conclave, and I was excluded like a poor relative to be pitied and teased.

She was careful to only share secrets I could never understand, but I didn't care, I hung on her every word. I just liked to be near her.

The fine sweat of exertion covered her face like a mist and her pupils were still dilated, like a wild animal caught unaware. The smell of hemlock root in the air was often used in their ceremonies. She was always manic, active and distracted after a Harridan congregation and this was no exception.

She spat as she saw me and shooed me away in irritation, but I just bided my time. She picked up her woollen cloak and wrapped it carefully around the thin purple voile that made up the ritual dress; the material torn by thorns and branches and hands in the fury of prayer. I admired every shred, every scar on her pale skin. She frantically pushed her hair to one side and quickly braided it, trying to tame the russet curls. She looked directly at me and nodded her head, she was ready to walk with me.

"You must stop watching us, Raykal." She spoke in her usual dismissive manner, but with an air of excitement tinged with superiority.

"Sorry Heligan, but I like to…" I hesitated, she wasn't listening anyway, her eyes were like black moons, none of the green hues shone through the thick pupils. She laughed, on the verge of hysteria and span around high on her toes.

"We searched the hieroglyphics today, only Ammute could touch the ancient scripts." She twisted around in circles as she spouted, "Oh, the beauty of those messages written long ago… So secret, so ambiguous." Her eyes now went into a hazy semi-trance, I knew not to ask any questions, but my mind was screaming with them.

"We found the bluebird; you could see the ruffle of its feathers scratched into the surface…" She continued and then stopped abruptly as if she'd suddenly realised something and came crashing down to earth. "I can't tell you what we saw, Raykal." Her cheeks glowed, and her saucer eyes laughed at me.

"I know…"

I so wanted to know the answer, the answer to everything. 'What would end the conflict between Tarnade and Nevisian?' An end to the feud would mean the return of my brother and in turn my mother's solace.

The war had been raging for two years now and we had not seen him in all that time. The reason for war was not lands or resources but the fact that the Nevisian elders did not believe the Harridans, as mere women, were able or resourceful enough to run a country.

The Nevisians were vulgar, violent individuals, who shared our borders and frequently committed raids; raping and killing our people. I was lucky enough to never have met one.

The Harridans were magical, but also harsh. They ruled with a rod of iron. The last rulers had been too disordered, the male leaders chose not to support rules or regulations and the people ran riot; it had been violent and chaotic. This all came to pass long before my birth, but my mother has told me stories of the time before the Harridans came to power.

"Have they found the answer? In the hieroglyphs? What about the maze?" I blurted out.

"The maze! What do you know about the maze, Raykal? You're not supposed to know!" She trailed off as a young man was striding toward us, head held high, an aura of confidence, urgency and beauty surrounded him.

It was Ethan. Heligan was in love with him, I knew this. But I also knew the Craft of Harridan did not allow its priestesses to be with a man. The priestesses were not allowed to marry or have a relationship of any kind as they believed it diluted the magic. It was an honour to be an Earth Mother, but as with all honours, there was also frustration and regret. Heligan had no time to tame her hair or adjust her dress, but her already animated face glowed.

"Hello to you both." Ethan spoke formally but with a glint of mischief. He was handsomely glorious with his abandoned blonde hair, tall and built like a young oak tree, with brown eyes you could melt into. He didn't look at me, his father would never allow him to have any association with my family.

Sadly, his mother had died in childbirth whilst being attended by my own mother. Ethan's father blamed my mother totally, even though it was his blind faith in the Harridans that failed her. He had not allowed her to be cut and so she had bled to death. Ethan in turn was a sickly baby and although he looked like a hero, he suffered from a breathing sickness that prevented him from fighting in the war. Instead he helped on his father's farm.

I took one glance at him and then lowered my head, but not without first noticing that he looked at every part of Heligan, almost breathing in the curves and sensuality of her body with boyish enthusiasm.

"You've been at the ceremony?" I think he recognised the black pits that were her pupils.

"Yes…" She didn't say it, she breathed it and a silence hung around the word like a chasm between them.

"Did you find what you were looking for, Earth Sister?" His tone was almost bitter, but the mischievous glint did not go away.

"Yes… I mean… No… We can't talk about it…" The meaningless words tumbled out miscellaneously. Ethan laughed and walked on, looked back and chuckled again.

Now that he had gone, it seemed colder. The breeze shifted and the trees hissed. Heligan pulled her cloak tighter around her and I huddled into my warm woollen coat. We undeniably missed his presence and continued to walk in silence. Heligan's eyes slowly cleared, the bottomless green returned, and the dancing stopped.

We separated at the entrance to my collection of huts. As I was an Unnamed, child of a Vermin, we lived outside the main community. Heligan waved as she made her way through the trees up the graded hill to her parental home.

As an apprentice, she did not yet live with the Harridans in the Fortress, not until she had passed all the initiation tests. I watched her for a moment, the red ringlets escaping from her plait and twisting in the wind. I admired the way her long legs carried her effortlessly up the bank.

I sighed, my heart full of longing and made my way down the cobbled path to my own worn and tattered thatched hut.

CHAPTER TWO
MY MOTHER

Once a Harridan herself, my mother had broken the rules by falling in love with my father. At the time she hadn't known that he had 'a wandering spirit'. She had told us about it once, muttering he could not stay in one place for too long and the call to move on had been abrupt. She had chosen to stay with us and that was all I had ever been told. We never mentioned him.

My mother was both revered and ostracised, being a psychic and midwife, and labelled as Vermin; a woman who is not married to a man and who has given birth to a child without a man by her side. It didn't bother her as it bothered me. She was not earth bound but instead consorted with the realm of fire and flames.

So, there she sat on the chair, handmade in wicker and plaited reeds, mesmerised by the flames. Her dark hair would have been wild if it wasn't tied away from her face. I had the same black hair, but always asked my mother to cut it short; lengthy hair got in the way, although I always kept my fringe long and floppy. My mother's most striking feature were her eyes.

At this moment they were shining sapphires, glinting in the fire's reflection. I was always jealous of them, mine were green and almond shaped but I had inherited her beautiful long lashes however lost they were on my muddy pools. We both had small noses but where her skin was clear and flawless, mine was sprinkled with freckles, caused, my mother said, by my compulsive love of being outside.

My mother watched the fire, looking for signs; she was known for reading the flames and people often came to her in times of trouble, looking for answers.

My mind wandered back to the night she received the prophecy...

She looked up as I entered the house and smiled a greeting, a wry, knowing smile with a hint of unpredictable madness. Cheese and bread were laid on the table, along with ale and water and I ate hungrily, feeding crumbs occasionally to Marples the cat hidden beneath the table. The cat was a ball of black fur with amber eyes and paws full of malevolent claws.

My mother turned back to the fire and suddenly grabbed a pen and the book beside her. She wrote automatically as if in a frenzy, like a poet who has been starved of inspiration for years only to rediscover it. I knew it was a message from the flames and that when she had finished, we would discuss it. We lived alone in a small cottage made of wattle and daub and roofed with thatch. It was simple and homely, but untidy as my mother was a hoarder of all things that could be useful, although very little of it was.

She made a living through her midwifery skills, along with psychic readings and healing; we lived well for people who were outcasts. Gallam was away fighting in the war and so our lives were spent in limbo waiting for news of him… Waiting like the rest of our community and the land of Tarnade.

My mother stopped writing and the pen and book fell from her hand. Her head dropped forward; she was exhausted from the trance-like experience. As always, I reacted quickly with a cup of cold water pressed to her lips to revive her. She would need time, but she would be fine. I glanced at the writing on the paper but could not decipher the scrawl, I would have to wait for her recovery.

It had begun to get dark outside and the twilight time of communication was ripe as our other worlds collided. Tarnade folk would be safe in their homes now sharing food and talking over the day. We tended not to venture out as this was the time for the Meads.

The Meads were mysterious wood nymphs; they lived separated from us in hidden places, in a parallel realm. I had glimpsed one only once; light and delicate and almost transparent. They moved quickly, often floating through the air like a dandelion seed and left no trail except for the scent of lavender, thick and clawing.

I don't think they were inherently evil, but they were mistrusted; if anything went missing it was blamed on the Meads, if you got ill then it was spread by the Meads. If anything was stolen, destroyed or someone had been injured, it was the Meads. In this way and in our suspicious society, they were known for being deceitful and treacherous creatures that were best left alone. Perhaps my mother and I had more in common with them than we thought, as we were outcasts on the edge of our community, mistrusted and belittled.

My mother came-to feeling refreshed, her sparkling eyes were bright and curious, her complexion back to its even blush. Even at the age of forty, she was very attractive and not only physically; she exuded a sense of excitement and unpredictability that intrigued men and women found strangely comforting. For someone who was ostracised by the community, my mother was popular for both her psychic readings and her knowledge of herb lore. Having once been part of the Earth Mother coven of Harridan, she was endowed with their knowledge and teaching and people sought it out. However, they did not include her or me in social gatherings, village meetings, decision-making or any part of community life.

The rules and conventions set by the Harridans were dubious — one member of our family is discarded whilst another, Gallam, is admired for fighting in the army, giving his life for a country that labelled his own mother and sister as contaminated and impure. It was a strange situation.

"Have you been to session today, Raykal? Or just hiding out at the castle?" My mother asked, but did not wait for an answer, as she already knew. "You need to attend," she continued, "it's your chance to be allowed back into the community and win a name." Her face contorted with concern.

Session was the school attended by the Unnamed. It was where we received instruction on historical law and behaviour; only those without fathers attended. We weren't trusted to have knowledge and behave like the other children, who attended normal school. We were disciplined with chains and evil slurs. It wasn't learning, it was torture. I was the only Unnamed in our small village, the others came from towns and villages spread around the area. None of the women wanted the stigma of an Unnamed child and to be outcast as a Vermin, they were careful.

If you passed the session, you were given the second name of 'Krim.' It was just another label, but it meant you could be accepted into the conventions of society – have a job, marriage, a chance, otherwise you were just hated forever.

"I don't want to mother… They are cruel to us, I prefer the comfort of the castle walls!" I protested.

A veil of worry fell over her, "It's your only chance to have a life, Raykal. You don't want to be an outcast all your life and the castle won't always be a sanctuary, not in these uncertain times." She was giving me one of those pleading looks, I knew she was right, but I didn't want to acknowledge this in my own mind. I changed the subject.

"Mother, the writing! What did you write? What message from the fire?" I looked at the writing book laid on the floor by the fire, almost forgotten.

"Oh yes!" She laughed and picked up the book. Her skirt rustling, she glanced over the scribbled page and her face changed to one of sadness and grief. I had never seen someone's face drop so much, her eyes creased, and her mouth took on a grim line of defeat.

"What is it?" I breathed, scared I might shatter the delicate silence that ensued.

"He's missing." Was all she said, but I knew exactly about whom she was talking, as if I had seen the crumpled note myself – my brother.

CHAPTER THREE
THE SKIMS

I had to go to session. I couldn't avoid it. I didn't want to upset my already weak and vulnerable mother; the news had hit her badly. I suppose she could ignore her own seeing, for that could be wrong, but not an official letter sent by messenger. She had a fitful sleep broken by murmurings and shallow breathing that kept me awake, or was it my own worry for her? After all, she was all I had now; no brother and no friend.

As I walked across the patchwork grasses, I could smell their meadow fragrance and it made my troubled spirit a little lighter. I passed the castle and I had to resist the temptation to spend the day in its comforting ramparts. Is it ironic to find a place with so much bloody history, so comforting? I made my way through the forest, past the Harridan groves, that when empty, still smelt of sacred herbs and extinguished fire pits. The trees I passed seemed burnished in texture and some were hollow; used by The Meads, creatures of the misty night, I knew I wasn't going to see one now, in the sharp frost of morning.

I looked up at the leaves, shaped like diamonds but softer, greener than emeralds, covered in dew, glossy and rich like velvet. These evergreens were a symbol of the Mother Earth and synonymous with the traditions and rites of our land.

The saying is that if the leaves fall from the tree then the power of the Harridans will also fall. This was a magical landscape we lived in, enchanted and beautiful but not without its scars. Trees had been hacked down in their prime and their logs strewn like severed limbs waiting to be used as resources on the battlefields. I realised it was not only humans that suffered in war; nature did too.

The heaviness of the burden I had woken up with this morning returned and, to add to my troubles, the school bell was tolling. The sessions took place in an old stone mill; the ancient brickwork caressed in ivy swirls, the windows were high up in the rafters so that they let in light but gave us inmates no chance to stare out of them and daydream. I entered through the vast stone doorway, which was carved with curses of the Vermin and their Unnamed; ever the reminder of who and what we were.

We sat in rows in silence on hard benches carved from trees, planks of oak still in the shape of the proud tree, the rough bark remained and every time we sat on them, we would get splinters. It was as if the tree was still protesting at being cut down in its prime, for such a hateful place and such a torturous reason. We stared ahead, looking at our teacher, who was dressed in a dull grey sack, known as a mantle cloak.

The Skims had only one job to do and that was to turn the Unnamed into useful and acceptable members of society. I could never understand how a child was to blame for their parents so-called mistakes, but this was how we were made to feel. They were generally evil, harsh and unfeeling, as if they had been programmed to be a certain way. They were not allowed to marry or have children or relationships of any kind and they were confined to the walls of the school. They used the grounds to grow what they needed to live. Their mantle cloaks were drawn around them by a belt which contained, what I can only describe as instruments of torture; a flexible stick of birch, a knuckle duster, an implement for nail pulling and a potion that once administered sent the victim into a sleep. A sleep that rendered one dizzy and nauseous for hours after. I knew this from experience. I was a constant disappointment and source of annoyance for the Skims and I was always in trouble – hence my desire to hide at the castle.

The day was regimented, which is probably what I struggled with most. I didn't take well to structure and authority but then again, I was told this was part of being an Unnamed and that I needed to change.

The day went like this: an hour of ancient history of Tarnade and its folklore and wars, its politics and how the Harridans came to rule. An hour of physical exercise.

An hour of scripture. An hour of law, inheritance and charnels. An hour of mind realignment. Oh yes, it was all about control.

In contrast, I was a dreamer, a believer in self-expression and other things I hadn't yet discovered but something told me they were out there somewhere.

There were physical punishments for rule-breaking and although I was no hero - I hated any form of pain - I seemed to be a regular target for punishment. The reason being both my passive and defiant attitude and that the Skims' inherent cruelty. The Unnamed, weren't seen as having the same minds or intellectual capacity as those born to normal parents. Our minds had to be improved, controlled even.

I wondered why my mother wanted me to go. On the other hand, I knew why - having a name was everything in our society. It was the only way to be accepted, to be no longer on the outskirts, an outsider, not able to get a job, marry the one you love or ask for help. My brother had struggled through all of this, had earnt himself a name to join the army and fight for his country. I always thought it ironic that he would give his life after all this torture, but perhaps that's what mind control does. I loved my brother, but we were very different. Yes, he was brave and strong but also more pliable and considered. I went with gut feeling.

It was during the hour of scripture that I began to lose focus. I had been fine during physical exercise but sitting for long periods listening to a constant drone of meaningless words did not appeal to me. The Skim had talked for half an hour about the sacred writing of Hilgard, the original founder of the Harridans, how their rule had brought back stability and contentment to a once war-torn place. 'Another piece of irony,' I thought, as we were at war and my brother was missing and no one seemed content.

It was when we were given a mind-numbing task to do that my mind wandered. I was thinking about Gallam and the moment when we were younger, when he tried to teach me sword fighting – with sticks. The memory was vivid, I remembered the sunlight had been streaming through the window of the castle. A vicious ray of light had blinded me, I lost concentration on protecting myself from the stick. I felt the blow across my hand, the pain was excruciating. He had put every ounce of strength he had into the blow – he was never careful with his little sister, he treated me as an equal. It was then that a real blow of pain rapped across my knuckles and I opened my eyes to see that a Skim had hit me with his own wooden stick.

"Wake up Vermin - no daydreaming allowed!" His long nose jerked as he spoke.

I screamed in pain and hugged my hand to my chest. Then remembered where I was and who I was, and I stared up defiantly at the ugly, stern uncaring face of the Skim.

"Work or you will continue to be the low life that you already are." He pointed the stick toward me, I flinched unwittingly and was instantly disappointed in myself as he placed the tip onto the paper in front of me.

"Do not look at me girl! Look at the paper, that's the key."

I stared into his face for one more second, taking in his sharp features; eyes that were black and dead and lips so thin they looked like scissor blades. That stare was my feeble attempt at rebellion. I looked down at the work and heard his scuffling steps as he went back to the front of the class.

The reddening welt on my hand was just another bruise to add to many accrued over my time here. I had made no real friends - we really were too scared to talk to each other, although occasionally we shared looks of horror or defiance. There were around thirty of us in this special school. Every one of us had different stories but we were all tarred with the same brush; sons and daughters of Vermin, the unmarried, the rule-breakers. We didn't exist in the scheme of things, we were unimportant, dirty, unwanted scum and such was the propaganda of the state that we believed it ourselves. All thirty of us believed ourselves to be worthless and in need of a name. A name would give us recognition and status and we could leave our sullied pasts behind.

I looked around the classroom, everyone had their heads bowed, shoulders hunched with no hint of pride or self-respect, well, not on the outside. Bullying was common in the school but worse in the community. The Unnamed tried to stay as quiet and inconspicuous as possible; there was no camaraderie here, no sticking together. I barely knew their names and we were not encouraged to communicate with each other. Everything was strictly overseen by the Skims and outside of school, we tended to be loners, not relying on or trusting anyone, even our own kind. Occasionally we acknowledged each other with a nod, or hello, or a short conversation, but there were no relationships; that is how the Harridans wanted it. We really were nobodies. This all changed when our names were finally earnt.

I caught the eye of Angel, a prickly girl, all thin and sharp featured, who managed to look cross and lost at the same time.

'Did she hate this as much as me? Did she think it was all wrong? What was her favourite colour, her favourite song, what were her hopes and dreams?' I could read nothing, her eyes were shut down, she blinked and looked down again and I was so in need of solace that I took the blink as a form of communication. She was saying, "Raykal, I hear you. Raykal, we *are* worth something. Raykal, we are friends." I looked back at my book and hoped it would all be over soon.

We had a short break before mind realignment and were allowed to sit or walk in the quadrant, a small square of greenery inside the school walls. The Skims, like prison guards, were on duty with whips in hand and hoods up over their heads. Grim reapers of the school yard. I wandered over to the water fountain and Angel was there too, wiping her thin lips with the back of her bony hand.

"Don't look at me in class again, Raykal." She said accusingly, her eyes narrowing.

"Sorry," I said, we looked at each other again. I'm sure for a second, I saw fire in her eyes, maybe she wasn't completely dead.

"I can't be looked at like that, you mustn't draw attention to me in any way." She looked genuinely scared, her emaciated face, even more tortured, if that was possible. "You've done it before." She added.

"Maybe... I'm sorry, it's just a need to make a connection with someone in there, we are all so separated."

"It's the way it has to be!" She hesitated before she continued "Especially for me..." She bowed her head a little. I got the distinct feeling that she wanted to tell me something. A Skim walked past. He looked directly at us.

"Drink then." Angel said, pointing to the water fountain. I did. I continued sipping the water until the Skim walked past.

"I really am sorry Angel, I feel that maybe we should all look after each other a bit more, not be so detached from each other. I mean we have a lot in common and we all hate the Skims."

At this point she stifled a sob, "No one will like me - there's no point."

"We all think that, but it can't be true! We all feel worthless, that's what we are made to feel, that getting a name is so important." I suddenly realised that this was the most conversation I had ever had with another Unnamed.

Strangely, it was with Angel, one of the most secretive and hostile among us, who now stood before me skeletal, dirty and crying. I didn't really know what to do. I looked behind me to see if any Skims would see and then put my arm tenuously around her shoulders. She seemed to freeze.

"Don't show me kindness Raykal. I don't want to feel what it's like, I don't want to get used to it or like it... You will hate me too when you know."

"Know what Angel? It can't be that bad, we are already hated and dismissed by society so how can it be worse? We're all in the same boat." I replied.

"It is worse for me." She wiped her nose with the back of her hand. "My father is a Skim."

My arm fell from her shoulders. My mind was in shock, trying to compute what she had just told me. 'Her father, a Skim? How awful, one of those foul evil torturers that made our lives hell.'

I had never seen Angel being treated in a favourable way. I've seen her being hit by both whip and ruler. No one had ever shown her a kindness or let her off work. I was confused. The horn was blown for end of break.

Putting my arm around her once again, I tried to reassure her. "Listen Angel, I don't hate you." I reached in my pocket and gave her my only hanky. "Meet me at the castle after mind realignment - we can talk there."

A Skim approached. "Move it girls, to the Great Hall... NOW!" We both moved quickly and didn't share another glance.

Mind realignment was always the last lesson before lunch. It was carried out in the large hall built from the same stone as the castle, probably stolen from the ruins of the great place. Mind realignment could range from forced meditation, chants and repetitions of laws, or even a public punishment. It was always led by the Master Skim.

This afternoon, there was a sense of anticipation in the hall, and the tension was palpable; dark, gloomy and negative. The Master Skelton, rapped his fingers on the oak desk in front of him, in a deliberately irritating way. I wondered, 'if they want us to gain a name, why do they always treat us with utter disdain and contempt?'

His face was a scowl, his dark eyebrows met in the middle of his forehead, seated above an overly large nose and a thin-lipped mouth that pointed downwards in sulky boredom. As we watched his face change with a sly smile, we all realised today's lesson would be punishment.

"Today..." his voice boomed, echoing around the Great Hall. He made the usual overly dramatic pause.

"We have another example of the hideous nature of the Unnamed and their Vermin families." He seemed to pick out individuals in the crowd, make eye contact and move on. "Who would want to be associated with the Unnamed, when they show they have no respect and add no value to our society?" Yet another dramatic pause and a look of contempt seeped in, amongst the sulky boredom on his face.

"We are gathered here to witness the punishment of Thomas the Unnamed. You will realise why you are all here, why it is essential to win a name and become citizens of Tarnade. Let me assure you that it is worth the struggle, it is worth the effort and it is worth the study to earn ultimate freedom within our world."

The Skims thought that the more times we were told about the importance of being named, the more it would condition our mind for it to be our goal. However, for me it just made me question how something so cruel, that tried to control people, was right.

As we stood through this, the people around me were shuffling nervously, no one liked these punishments, as they knew it could easily be one of them up there. Thomas was brought in with a rope around his neck. His head was down, so as not to look at any of us. We, on the other hand, were not allowed to keep our heads down, we were made to watch – it was all part of the 'mind control' and obviously a punishment had more effect if it was etched in detail in our minds.

"What, indeed, has this boy done, I hear you ask?" The Master Skelton blathered on. I didn't hear anyone asking or caring what he had done. I looked around for Angel and saw her at the front, looking up at the scene compliantly.

"This boy has deviously tried to break into our vaults and steal a name certificate, without earning it!" A long pause followed. Not one sound was heard from his audience, no gasp of horror or sigh of disappointment, which showed that nobody cared that he had broken any rules, but they cared greatly that he was going to suffer.

I, personally, was relieved and hopeful that there were some of us that were prepared to take a stand, that had the guts to take a risk. I realised it was probably desperation, after years of bullying from the Skims and pressure from his mother that made him do it.

They took the rope from around Thomas' neck, pushing him against a large wooden pillar in the centre of the hall stage. They then used the rope to fix his arms around the pillar, so his face was kissing the smooth wood. They cruelly pulled off his shirt and exposed his back. A Skim took out the whip from his special belt and wacked the back of poor Thomas with so much fury that you could hear the whip as it travelled through the air. The horror was only heightened by Thomas' scream as it hit his skin and tore into its softness. The whole room seemed to wince at the same time. I took a sharp intake of breath, as if I was experiencing the pain for him. We all were, that was the whole point, and what the Skims wanted us to feel. The second lash made a cut parallel to the first and a line of blood seeped from the wound.

I closed my eyes only for a Skim to whisper in my ear that closing your eyes was not allowed and would put me in line for my own punishment. His whisper was sinister, and I could smell his foul breath, so I had to open my eyes again and look at the torture. Maybe, the mind conditioning was working, no one likes pain or the thought of it. I obeyed and did as I was told and at the end of the punishment I too turned away from the patterned red lines on Thomas' back and thought I was lucky that it wasn't me and I'm sure Angel did the same, but to be associated through blood to one of these torturers, yes it was worse for her... I turned and made my way home, I couldn't stand any more.

As I walked, I thought deeply about why nobody stood up to the Skims and their torture and harsh discipline. This loathing quickly turned inwards, I accused myself of weakness and of being a coward. I knew it was true, I wasn't brave like my mother, or my brother or maybe my father; I was just a nameless little girl.

I looked down at my hand, it still smarted from the hit and the throbbing was like repeated taunts of mocking reproach of all that I was. I couldn't stand it and tears began to form.

I heard clumping footsteps behind me. It was Flynn, one of the other Unnamed. He was slightly out of breath as he caught up to me, his body waddling from side to side, "I couldn't wait to leave either, Raykal. I can't stand that mind realignment but if you abscond... You have to pay." It took him longer to speak because he was struggling for breath.

I really could not be bothered to talk to him, I probably should have been more understanding, he was after all, an Unnamed like me and he and his mother went through daily attacks, as we did; his even worse perhaps because he was bullied for his weight.

"I know," I reluctantly replied. "But have you ever thought, Flynn, that the punishment... is sometimes worth it?"

"No, the punishment is never worth it... Ever." He rushed past me. "I only have fifteen minutes to get back!" He shouted over his shoulder.

Looking ahead at Flynn, as his short fat legs trundled along, I did wonder if there was a spark in me, like there was in Thomas, somewhere deep down. 'Did I want to be a rebel? There must be more than this?' Then I looked down at my red hand, held it gently in my other and made my way to the castle, my safe place.

Angel wasn't there, and I wondered whether she would come, would she have the nerve to come? I perched on what must have been some sort of altar stone, it was now toppled to one side but sturdy enough to sit on. I really wasn't hungry after what I had just seen but I got out my bread and cheese anyway. I looked at it but couldn't eat it.

I heard footsteps and looked up to see the slight figure of Angel in the doorway.

"I wasn't sure you would come." I said, making room for her on the crumbled altar.

"Nor was I, especially after seeing what they did to Thomas." She sat next to me and I offered her some bread, which she accepted but only picked at. We sat in silence for a while, the breeze rustled through the growing weeds on the walls and the birds chirped out their songs from the surrounding trees and all was peaceful.

"It's nice here." Angel spoke nervously. "About what I said earlier, I feel I do need to tell someone, but can I trust you Raykal, can I?" Her high-pitched voice shook.

"Yes of course, we all have our secrets and problems." I reassured.

"You think of the Skims as cold and evil?" Angel continued, "That they torture and treat us with disdain, yes?"

"Yes, that is all I have ever seen them do Angel." I replied.

"Do you know who they are? Where they come from - anything about them? I doubt it… After all a Skim is a Skim. Why would you care?" Her voice had stopped shaking and I realised that what she said was true. I knew nothing about them, only that they existed; they had a job to do and they followed it through with cruelty.

Angel continued with some passion, "They are not innately evil Raykal, they are people that have gone against

Harridan rule. A lot of them are made up from the society of men that used to rule here, or from rebels or those who have broken the rules. It's what the Harridans do to rule-breakers, they imprison them in the dark, so their skin goes sallow, they starve them of nutrients and light, they burn off their hair, they torture them and give them drugs that keep them under their control. That's what the Skims are... They are rebels!"

Her words shocked me to my core. These evil beings were once normal people of Tarnade, with families, friends, a job and a life, but because they stood against the Harridans, they were changed, tortured, drugged and spelled. I couldn't believe it, it made me see the Harridans in a different light. I knew they were controlling and hard, but I thought, as most did in Tarnade, that they did it for the right reasons. I never thought they would use their magic to harm. I didn't know what to think.

Angel continued, "My mother told me that father rebelled, he was with a small group of men that tried to rescue some miners caught up in a collapsed mine. They became trapped but the Harridans said there was nothing that could be done. My father felt that they had turned their backs on them. Some of the rebels left Tarnade and escaped but my father and a couple of others were arrested, and after several years in prison, they became Skims."

"Do you know who your father is... which Skim?" I asked gently, I didn't want to upset her more.

"No, he is unrecognisable, and as my mother says, not the same man as he was. They must wipe their memories or dull them or something... Maybe your father too, Raykal?"

The thought had not occurred to me, but it chilled me to the bone. I knew nothing of my father. I remember Gallam asking questions, but it just upset my mother so much he stopped asking, and I too picked up on this and just never asked.

"I don't know anything about my father Angel... I just don't know... There's so much to think about and so much to take in." I really was confused and stunned. My answer seemed to panic Angel, the shake came back to her voice.

"I shouldn't have told you... You must hate me! I am a Skim!" She looked so downcast, so small, so rejected, I reached out and touched her hand and she let me.

"I do not hate you, you are not a Skim, even your father is not a Skim. They are beings created from torture, cruelty and addiction and it is no wonder that is all they know. I'm not going back there. Never!"

"But Raykal, you need a name – I need a name, my mother says if I get a name, I will somehow restore my father's pride... I don't know how but I have to try and I hope beyond hope, that one day there will be a flicker of recognition in a Skim's eye, even if he is beating me or shouting at me... That is what I want more than anything." Angel's eyes glimmered with a light then, a light of hope.

"I'm not sure I want one of their names now." I was sure of that, it meant nothing to me.

"If you do not get a name you may well be considered a rebel and become a Skim." The thought obviously scared her to death, as the fear in her face was clear. It made me afraid too, and so confused.

"I've got to go now Raykal, thank you for everything. Please, no more glances at me, no looks of sympathy at school. No one must know. I must do my time and get my name, do you understand?" The hard coldness was back in her eyes.

"Yes, I understand." I let go of her hand and she walked away.

All I could do was watch and try and calm my thoughts. I reached into my pocket and brought out my stone, it exuded its green and gold heat and I held it tightly up to my lips and whispered, "Please, please don't let my father be a Skim."

CHAPTER FOUR
THE HARRIDANS' SEARCH

After Angel left, I decided to stay on at the castle rather than go home. I had too much on my mind and I felt change all around me. The castle felt like a safe haven, a kind of solace that I didn't get at home and deep inside I didn't want to face my mother's grief over Gallam.

The sun was thinking about setting, it glowed low in the sky. I knew the time was right for a ritual and I decided to spy. I had always been interested in the surreptitious Harridan rituals. They gave me a chance to see Heligan, and she in turn accidently revealed pieces of information that made me want to know more. I wanted to know about how the coven was structured, how it was run and most importantly, the 'secret' they were constantly looking for.

'Why was this secret so important?' My mind was filled with questions. I needed to know.

If I climbed the crumbling tower, there was a slit window with a ledge, just wide enough for me to sit on, even though it was precarious.

From this window, I could get a reasonable view of the Harridan's forest Ritual Glade. I could now recognise the individuals and their roles by the colour of their robes.

Obviously, we were taught the Harridan history at school and how they had saved Tarnade from a time of confusion and anarchy, where laws were few and society was left to run itself into the ground. Morals were ignored and people did what they thought was right. Fighting often broke out between one man and another or one faction and another. The Harridans wrote down the rules and organised society. Sick of mistreatment at misogyny, the Harridans used their powerful knowledge and magic to take over. However, the rituals and the cult of Harridan didn't feel like a heroic attempt to save the country. It was more about power, control and a desire for something just out of reach.

The ritual glade was littered with heather in shades of mottled brown. The oaks stood like guardians, some like knights, with their swords raised as if turned to wood at the moment of charge. That would be typical of the Harridans, not to turn the brave enemy to stone as someone could surely turn them back again, but instead, to turn them to wood, so they could live on bound by bark and leaf, only husks of their former glory and unlikely ever to be restored.

The place had an intense feeling of sadness as the lush green grass was littered with rotting wood, grey and lifeless like discarded bones in an elephant's graveyard.

The debris of fallen trees struck by storm winds in the height of winter and lightning in the electrical storms of summer. Life, however, was in the twisted limbs of the oaks themselves as sap like blood pumped through the fibres. The sap of the oak was known for its healing qualities and used in many medicines. However, what interested the Harridans more was the sap of the Yew tree - poisonous to those that misused it.

A silence suddenly descended on the glade, even the wind dropped to stillness and I knew the ritual was about to begin.

The procession of the Harridans began, and I crooked my neck to get a better view. The Harridans have a hierarchical structure, this is reflected in everything they do, including ritual. There are the lower orders, those that are in training - like Heligan - they stood between the oaks and started reciting the ritual prayer in low voices so that it sounded like a low purring hum.

The next Harridans to appear were the middle orders, those who are fully qualified and have passed all the tests, these are the workers - the ones that keep everything ticking over. Recognised by their green robes with hoods pulled over their heads. They carried wooden torches to light the ritual fire in the middle of the clearing. As the flames rose the chanting became louder and the novices raised their arms above their head as if encouraging the flames to rise higher and higher. The workers encircled the flames and bowed down on their knees.

It is at this point that the elders and leaders appeared, led by Ammute their leader - the epitome of female strength. She held a hint of unpredictable cruelty, she could never be trusted and was always feared. Her long grey wavy hair, half plaited in the Harridan style, flowed freely without any covering and her very youthful body for she must have been seventy years at least. She wore the darkest red with a gold shimmering hue that hinted of the forest itself. This enhanced her amazingly green eyes, that stood out like jewels from the craggy lines and crevasses of her face. She had an aura of certainty, as if she had experienced enough to know everything, but also had the strength of mind to destroy whomsoever she looked at. In fact, her skills in hypnotising were well known and it was said, she had used it to hold on to her position and how she negotiated with other powers. She was followed closely by her Sisters... Four of the highest trained Harridans who made up the senior conclave. Lahore, Mintel, Hesta and Megan were all very close and each had an expertise for which they were respected.

Lahore was around forty years old and was an expert in the 'Magic arts for the power of good'. She knew spells and incantations that could raise spirits and control people.

Mintel was the youngest of the conclave, only recently joining, it was said that she could make any potion that was needed to keep someone alive or indeed kill them. A fascination with chemistry had enabled her to study her art, making her invaluable to the Harridans and their pursuit of power.

Hesta was the peoples' Harridan. She was the one that recruited apprentices and acted as an intermediary between the Harridans and the people of Tarnade. She also issued the proclamations and propaganda.

Lastly, there was Megan, the priestess with very similar talents to my mother, a medium and connector to the otherworld. The Harridans did nothing without referring to Megan and her spirit voices. Her appearance was so distinctive, her hair and skin were almost pure white and her eyes, in contrast, a deep blue with the blackest of limbal rings around the iris.

She wore a crystal band down her centre parting with an onyx crystal sharpened to a point. This gave her an angular sharp appearance and a real coldness in her eyes as if they looked straight through you.

The rituals of the Harridans are secret and only for the select few. I knew more than I should, spying on them from the castle parapets and the forest edge. From what Heligan whispered to me in moments of heightened drug use or just in excitement, I knew that the Harridans were looking for an answer to something - I just didn't know what.

A fire was lit in the centre of the clearing and a circle of fresh-faced young Harridan apprentices linked arms and danced around the fire whilst the sparks of light took hold. I thought I could just make out Heligan's russet curls and lithe body dancing enthusiastically. It was important to the Harridans that each element of nature was included in the rites. Fire was always the beginning and Water was always the end; as they poured sacred water from the consecrated springs onto the fire to put it out.

The dancing stopped and a gap was made as the apprentices lifted their arms up to the sky. Megan walked through the gap and called on the fire spirits to enhance the flames, she then took an intake of breath and blew onto the now ferocious fire. My view of her was stolen by a plume of flame and smoke. As it cleared, she stood there, eyes closed and unaffected.

In her hands was a torch made of chestnut wood; which doesn't burn too quickly but gives off a steady light. A prayer to the element of Air was said, in low voices like the hum of a thousand bees; "May the great Spirit of the Air, life giver and freedom dancer, purify our minds with an intake of wisdom and light. May our thoughts become lucid, keen and radiant, so that we can find the answer and the golden age will dawn among us."

At this moment, Ammute came forward and took the torch from Megan. "Earth my body, water my blood, air my breath and fire my spirit." The apprentices threw earth on to the fire chanting in whispers at first, again and again getting louder and louder, building to a crescendo until Lahore stepped forward. In her hand, the root of the Mandragora steeped in moon water. The twisted thick roots of the Mandragora were known to be poisonous but steeped into the water and then drunk, the root enhanced the senses and made the Harridans more conscious both spiritually and physically. Lahore passed the bowl around the circle of apprentices and then the general circle. As the liquid became more concentrated with Mandragora it was passed to the senior conclave and lastly, Ammute took the piece of root left in the bowl and placed it into her mouth.

The warmth of the fire seemed to heat the group and there was more freedom of movement, their bodies contorted into shapes that matched the flames and the mellow buzz of chants were replaced by shouting for the gods of nature and deep throaty cries were offered into the air. Cloaks were thrown off to reveal the delicate tulle dresses that moved with the fluidity of water. Hair that was plaited and tamed escaped confinement and caught in the wind. As the Harridans danced, the wooden book of the Hieroglyphs was brought towards Ammute, touched by many hands. The Hieroglyphs were sacred writings from the ancestors, that only the Harridans could read in their heightened state of understanding.

It was difficult to see any detail of the scripts from where I was high up in the castle, but I could see as the book was opened that there were scraps of a document and the pages were ragged, tattered and some pieces had been sewn back together. How someone could read that I didn't understand.

Ammute held it high in the air, then many chestnut torches were held around her as she lowered the book and began reading, words that I neither recognized nor understood.

"Haratha, nembulis, Cathridal, isssh," it began. I had watched the ritual several times and it always started off the same way. Ammute would then choose a page and spend time studying it and reading it aloud as the other Harridans listened. Sighing and wailing were common which broke the silence. Heligan said something about using the collective energy of them all to help loosen the knowledge needed.

It was then that Lahore brought forward the map and it was rolled out in front of Ammute, it was called The Maze; I knew this from what Heligan had told me. The Maze was a warren of underground tunnels, rock deposit sites and old mines that entwined the three districts we knew about – Tarnade, Navisian and Eviss. The Harridans were looking for something, that was obvious, but no one, apart from the inner conclave knew what.

This time Mintel brought forward a torch of fire and waved it over the maze and the Harridans rose from their positions and held hands in a circle around the map and hummed in a low tone as Ammute walked the maze until she felt she should stop. She knelt and placed a marker at that point. Lahore wrote down the coordinates in a small black book.

"The search party will now leave." Ammute spun round and randomly pointed around the circle and one by one the green clad dancers moved forward.

When six were chosen, each were given a sacramental knife, I guessed for protection, and a saddled horse, which they mounted. The leader of the group was given the co-ordinates, with a map and they moved off galloping into the twilight.

I leaned back against the wall. It was over now, the Ammute and the four sisters being the first to leave, followed by the other Harridans, eyes still wide with drug induced excitement. What with Angel's news and this spectacle I was both thoughtful and confused. Questions spun in my mind. 'Were the Harridans evil?'

We knew they were harsh and ordered, but I, my mother and even Heligan never thought they were evil, otherwise they would not have joined the craft.

'What are they looking for?' My natural curiosity cried out to know.

I climbed down from the parapet and wondered if it was worth waiting for Heligan as I usually did, but something had changed since I'd witnessed her secret embrace with Ethan.

I decided too much had happened today and I couldn't face anything else. I made my way home alone and the impending darkness, like a shadow, followed me.

CHAPTER FIVE
THE MARKET PLACE

My mother's walk through the Market was either disturbed by people asking her for advice or booking her for healing. Sometimes she returned with rotten fruit juice spilling down her dress or a cut from a thrown stone. It was an inconsistent life and she didn't want me to suffer the same fate.

Today, I had decided to accompany her, partly to take my mind off the issues of Heligan and Angel. Also, my mother seemed more vulnerable than usual, the news about my brother had taken its toll and she hadn't been sleeping, her eyes were bagged, and her mouth drawn into a resolute line. Her head bent slightly forward stretching her neck as if she were determined to carry on. I think if she didn't have to look after me, she would not have ventured into the market.

As we turned the corner a scruffy, unkempt woman clutching her shawl around her shoulders, even though it wasn't too cold, hurried towards us. I took a step back and could see the hesitation in my mother's eyes.

'What was this woman going to do?' There was no greeting from her, only look of desperation as she spoke.

"My daughter's showing signs of birthing, can you come later today?" We both relaxed. My mother was often asked to help with births. The Harridans demanded payment for their services, a donation to the cause. They always got what they asked. People felt safe with them, they were the experts, the authority and the chosen ones. People thought nothing could go wrong if a Harridan attended a birth, they saw it as divine intervention.

However, those who had very little or nothing could not use them without losing part of their meagre livelihood and so they called on my mother or other healers. My mother said she would attend the birth and we moved on.

The Marketplace buzzed like a beehive. Everyone seemed to have a purpose, the noise was bursting and there were smells and tastes in the air that made you feel hungry, then sick and transported you to far off worlds.

The clash of a hammer against steel reverberated as the Waggoner fixed the wheels. The baker, with a face stained red form the heat cursed and turned the air purple with orders. The baked bread smelt of sweet oats, the uncooked dough balls felt like pillows of cloud. The mouldy stench of cheese filled your nostrils as you past the dairy stall. 'How could something that smelt so bad, taste so good?' The goats cheese melted on your tongue and the cow's milk cheese exploded with creaminess.

My favourite of all was the Alchemy stall. There was a uniquely glorious smell as we approached; full of deep sensuous spices, then the colours hit you, liquids of so many different hues sparkling in their vials, beautiful but menacing as half of them could kill as well as cure. This very power appealed to me, along with the sense of excitement of which these potions spoke of. Worlds that I had never heard of, but so wanted to know about.

Master Taliesin was the travelling chemist, who every year or so with his cart, set up camp. I found him fascinating. He looked old before his time, such a craggy face that was so full of lines and crevices and scars that you couldn't stop staring at. Each frown mark was like looking at an ancient map with lost roads telling a thousand stories. He wasn't known for his joviality or friendliness, but he was known far and wide for his knowledge, and knowledge was one of my favourite things. He was often seen running his hands over the bottles and muttering to himself. Whilst doing this, his eyes sparkled. Hidden in the muddy green was a catalyst of yellow light that ensnared and hypnotised. Those eyes spoke of long sea voyages, with crashing waves and violent spray. They spoke of trade with tribal peoples, of dusky nights and deserts of moving sand. Exotic food and intoxicating liquids, carved totems with the thud of dancing feet and the deep throated calls of wild places.

When Taliesin caught me watching him, he would call me over and let me hold a vile. He would take out the cork and tell me to sniff and there was either a beautiful waft of summer meadows, bursting with mimosa flowers or a stench that would make you wince, as it fried your nasal cavities with its strength. Sometimes, it would be a smell that took you back home to the comfort of the womb.

"How is this created?" I would ask, and he would smile, then a thousand more creases would encircle his features and he would laugh and talk of the magic of the Inca's, the Margerams and the tribal herbs they used. This would only serve to ignite my curiosity further and I would wonder, my imagination creating images from his words and time would literally be lost.

Today, he offered me a purple vial, he smiled his usual craggy way.

"Smell it." He urged pushing it toward me. I always did as he said. I trusted him wholeheartedly.

The smell was heady and rich; it smelled of lavender but, in my mind, heightened feelings of earthiness, mixed with the bark of trees and the essence of fresh air.

I sighed and Taliesin laughed. "Do you recognise it child?" He goaded.

"It's like I've smelled it before, but I can't remember." I wracked my brain. Not wanting to disappoint him.

"On an evening breeze perhaps?" He raised his eyebrows and some of the deeply etched lines disappeared, for a moment.

"I... Don't know," I hesitated. Yes, I recognised the aroma, but it was also mysterious to me, I couldn't quite place it but so wanted to as Taliesin would be pleased, and I liked to please him.

"It's essence of the Meads child - the fairy creatures that inhabit our woodland glades."

"Ah yes I know, we are told to go inside if we smell this, as the Meads can cause you to get lost or steal from you. I have never seen one as a whole only a wisp of their vapour. I must admit I am curious - have you seen them Taliesin? Have you?" I could see by the contortion of his lips and the added twinkle in his eye that he had indeed had a close encounter with a Mead.

"Yes, yes I count them as my friends." He waved his hand dismissively. I was shocked, most people in Tarnade hated them, the Harridans had warnings out about them everywhere. I think Taliesin sensed my concern; you couldn't keep much from this man.

"Child there is much we could learn from these creatures, it is people's own fear of the unknown that keeps our cultures apart, that and the mis-sold propaganda of our times!" Taliesin seemed to lose track and a sense of sadness enveloped him. "No, indeed, they are misunderstood, so misunderstood." He inhaled deeply of the lavender scent and replaced the lid, caressing the bottle fondly, he placed it back in his leather belt, where he kept the potions he held most dear.

He patted me affectionately on the shoulder. "Maybe one day you will get to meet a Mead and learn from them Raykal." His eyes turned a shade darker as they always did when Taliesin knew something others didn't.

"Here's your mother now." I looked around and couldn't see her, but Taliesin could probably feel her presence way before I could. I thought about the Meads and the possibility of meeting one and felt myself shiver, both with trepidation and excitement.

My mother always knew where to find me. With a basket full of cheese, vegetables and bread, she came over and placed her hand gently on Taliesin's arm, as if there was an understanding between them. I guessed they both knew about the essence of things. My mother walked away from the stall and I reluctantly followed. The air was still, no breeze caught in my hair, my mind was still cascading with thoughts of the mysterious and the exotic. My mother turned to wave to Taliesin but as she turned her head back around, a stone caught her forehead and a trickle of blood ran like an undammed river down her face. I grabbed her hand, as I heard a scathing voice call out: "Scum!" My mother wiped the blood with the back of her hand and carried on stoically walking. No one would have known she felt any emotion or fear, she kept her head down and just held my hand more tightly. I, however, looked up defiantly at the older woman and saw a look of disgust on her face. I returned her look with one of hatred. The woman spat on the ground as we passed. Despite the crowded and bustling market no one uttered a word in our defence or stirred to protect us.

Everything continued around us, as if we were in a slow-motion bubble, not really existing in their world.

A terrible rage bubbled inside me, I wanted to scream and shout and make them listen. I wanted my mother to fight, draw a sword on them, or use her sharp tongue. But no, we walked on by, as we always did when this happened. It was one of those things to be expected and endured.

My mother, a healer and midwife with skills and kindness, being treated as dirt. Heligan trapped into a contract that maybe meant giving up the boy she loved or facing god knows what and Angel, an Unnamed herself, tortured by the knowledge that her father was imprisoned and changed into something she would never recognise.

Inside, I felt that I was just as good as anyone else, despite my beginnings but in this society, what you felt was best kept inside and I did not have the confidence to speak my truth yet.

I think it was in that moment; induced by the smell of adventure and the reality that I did not belong, that I decided to go and find my brother, even before my mother asked me to.

CHAPTER SIX
THE QUEST IS SET

The attack in the Marketplace seemed to signify the end of my mother's fight to carry on. She tossed and turned in her sleep calling my brother's name as if he was just in front of her. I lay awake listening, worried that she wouldn't wake up from whatever nightmare suffocated her. When she did awake, she was sweating and crying. My mother had always been the strong one, well she had to be, she was the only one. She dwindled into illness, a sort of melancholic longing, that ate away at her energy.

There was no longer soup on the stove or bread to eat. The house was looking sorry for itself, and the garden weeds were choking the vegetables. I was worried. She stayed in bed or rocked incessantly on the chair by the fire, watching the flames, waiting, wanting the sight to return to her, but it was as if she wanted it so much, she was blocking it.

"I refuse to believe that he is dead," is all she said, whispering to herself as if it was a chant from a spell or mystical refrain created to bring back life.

My mother had built a shrine to Gallam in the corner of the room, it is what she was trained to do as a Harridan.

When someone was missing, you kept their spirit alive in their belongings, the objects their energy was captured in. There was his old leather gillet, an old coin and a book on ancient heraldry. Along with a pile of chestnuts from his favourite tree. All this surrounded a large tin goblet, blackened by the burning of incense that had to be tended both day and night, if the smoke stopped peppering the air, then it was believed that that person's life force also came to an end.

My mother collected the cones and herbs like clockwork for the incense but forgot to collect food for us. Keeping my brother alive was killing her, I hadn't seen her eat for days and her face looked taut and emaciated. As the sight seemed to have deserted her, she looked for news in other ways, another letter, gossip, word of some sort. Nothing ever came, it was driving her mad.

She slept fitfully, taking naps when she felt too ill or tired to carry on. Then she had another nightmare, as usual she tossed and turned and whispered and cried out. She woke up with a start, her eyes large and wide as if she had seen a massacre. She called out to me and I went and patted her hair and fetched a cold cloth to bathe her forehead. As I went to put the cooling pad to her skin, she grabbed my hand. "I need to tell you … about your … father."

"He, Ragan, was broad and strong with shocking red hair and a wide smile that pulled you in, with green eyes, like yours Raykal, that reflected strength of character and goodness and rebellion." Her eyes glistened, she smiled mistily as she said these words, her voice was croaky as if it took a lot of strength to speak but this cleared and came through much stronger and proud. "He was a renegade, a non-conformist, he was outspoken about the Harridans and their control, he was a realist, but he believed in equality. He wasn't perfect, but he had passion!" She stopped for a moment as if to catch her breath. "They ousted him from society when he tried to raise a protest for the mine workers. When I met him, he worked at the Geode mine and conditions were not good." She continued, "there was an accident, ten men were trapped, Ragan and some others tried to rescue them, they tried to get help but all the Harridans would do was close the mine and pray for their souls. He came to the realisation that everyone in this society was uncared for and persecuted, he became depressed. He couldn't stay here..." It was as if her mind had begun to wander. "He had a restless soul, he wanted to find a better place, as this one was not open for change."

All I could think was 'why didn't you go with him?'

I remembered what Angel had told me about her father and I wondered if they once knew each other and I also felt a sense of relief that my father got away – at least he isn't a Skim!

"I couldn't" my mother continued, "I was young, my mother was ill, she needed me and I didn't know when I said goodbye that I was pregnant with Gallam. As he walked away, I thought my heart would break."

I had never seen such sadness in her eyes, and I realised why she never spoke about him.

"Obviously I lost my place with the Harridans and only escaped punishment as my mother had left me some money so I paid my way out."

"He came back four years later, to find me, I was labelled 'Vermin' by then and he was devastated by the poverty and disgrace he had left me in. He wanted to stay and marry me but by this time he was labelled as a troublemaker. He was harassed by the people under instructions of the Harridans, he hid in your old castle, but they were looking for him, they wanted him gone. I couldn't go with him." The voice of regret continued, "I had a small four-year-old boy, your father was just a traveller, he had no means, just getting work where he could. Also, he told stories of plagues and worst places. So I stayed and he was run out of town. Banished and cursed by the very group I used to belong to. It broke my heart and then you came along..."

She looked directly into my eyes, so far was she buried in the past.

"The guilt at bringing another Unnamed into the world was overwhelming, but you Raykal were a product of love, there was no denying that. My life is you and Gallam." My mother's eyes filled with tears, about to burst, "Until I know Gallam is safe I will wither away. Raykal." She grabbed my hand hard and squeezed it until the blood left my fingers. "You must go and find Gallam and bring him back to me. My sight has deserted me, but I know that you are strong and determined, like your father. Am I asking too much?" She looked deep into the depths of my eyes searching for the answer from my soul, instead of my lips. I knew my soul was saying yes. In fact, I felt secure in the knowledge that it was the right thing to do, but at the same time I was excited by an adventure and scared senseless.

Suddenly, my feelings overwhelmed me. I had to escape from the imprisonment of her grief, I had to do something.

I decided to go and see if Taliesin was still in town, he often slept in his covered cart when the market closed late. I made sure my mother was asleep and that the goblet was still smoking, she would never forgive me if that went out. I was nervous at leaving the house as the sun had gone down and I knew it was the time of the Mead's trickery, also there was the danger of attack, as an Unnamed I was a target. But the claustrophobia of the cottage, the smell of sickness, incense and the whirl of information in my brain had got to me - I needed an escape and someone to talk to.

The evening was drawing in, the sun had set and the there was a denseness about the atmosphere which matched my thoughtful mood. I walked quickly and took deep breaths of air, both to refresh my lungs and so I could decipher if any mischievous Meads were near. I found Taliesin's cart parked on a grassed area just to the side of the market. I could see the back of his head as he sat gazing into the fire watching a pot of something cooking on a make-shift tripod. There was no noise apart from the crackle of the flames and the gentle steaming of the pot, a part of me didn't want to disturb him. But then I did need him, I walked nearer and without turning his head Taliesin spoke. "I knew you would come tonight child...come and sit."

I smiled to myself, only Taliesin would know it was me without even looking.

I went and sat opposite him and studied his craggy, uneven face and felt immediately calmer and confident.

"You are most welcome to join me, but can I ask why you have come?" My instinct told me that he already knew why, but I went along with the game.

"My mother has, for the first time, told me about my father. I need someone to talk to - I have no friends." I hesitated. I thought of Angel or Heligan – then thought of her with Ethan, to me she had changed alliances and yes, I had to admit I felt betrayed, but I couldn't stop myself from loving her.

"No, you should never stop loving her." Said Taliesin.

I jolted out of my thoughts and realised he was reading them. I didn't feel invaded - I just accepted it and smiled, his voice was low and steady and it calmed my spirit.

"You know everything Taliesin?" I asked.

"No child, I don't know everything, far from it, but I know some things, yes... some things."

"What do you know about my father? Did you meet him?" I asked this nervously as I really didn't know if I was ready to learn any more.

"Yes, he was a good man, a kind man, a man that sacrificed much to be free and search for the truth. You have his heart Raykal, I know that much, and it will serve you well on your journey...yes." He paused and then reached for a large wooden spoon and a small carved wooden bowl "Have some food child."

"You know I have to go on a journey to find my brother. My mother has asked me." I put out my hands in anticipation of the bowl of food.

"Yes, she asked but you had already decided with the throw of the stone and even before that you knew you were not set for a life here in Tarnade – this is true is it not Raykal? You rebel against getting a name and you are far too inquisitive - watching all from those castle walls eh?" He handed me the bowl as if he were handing me a lifeline and I accepted, it smelled so good.

I knew from that point that Taliesin knew my soul, he knew it all, more than he was telling me, but I also knew I had to learn that part for myself. The crackling bright flames confirmed this and I suddenly felt at peace with not knowing.

"I have to travel on tomorrow to the market at Murrin," Taliesin spoke between mouthfuls of rich rabbit meat and wild garlic stew. "I will not be able to see you off, but I wish you hope on your journey - remember that suffering is part of learning Raykal and that questioning what is right is part of the journey of life. Do not live by what you know, but instead live by what you learn from others." His eyes shone bright like miniature stars in the darkening sky.

"You hold a stone with you Raykal?" I looked curiously at him for a moment, not quite comprehending what he said.

"Oh yes," I had forgotten for a moment about my stone. I reached into my pocket and brought out the stone, "Just a silly trinket that I carry, like a talisman, to wish me luck and help me reflect on how grateful I should be for what I have." The mere smoothness of the stone on my fingers comforted me.

"Let me see child." I handed the stone to Taliesin and in his fingers, it seemed to glow even greener, or was it the light of the fire, that made the green and yellow swirls dance.

"This is no normal stone... it is ..." He paused and I thought I glimpsed tears in his eyes or was it the fire playing tricks again.

He swallowed, "It is a unique stone from a special place - it will mean more to you than you think child, take care of it and it will take care of you." He continued to stare at the stone in his fingers, holding it up to the light, he didn't seem to want to let it go and was lost in it for a while. He coughed and brought himself back to reality, where he handed the stone back to me and I placed it, with a bit more care than before into my pocket. If it meant something to Taliesin, it must be special.

I didn't pretend to understand what he said, but something told me that it was right and the meaning would become clear along the way. We continued to sit around the fire. I ate the stew with gusto as we had not had much more than bread and cheese lately. Taliesin made me laugh with stories of his own travels and dancers in rainbow silks and kings with large stomachs trying to win back lost kingdoms. I didn't want to move but Taliesin himself got up and began to clear away.

"That incense is about to burn away child." Was his warning, I knew it was time to return home. I said goodbye, he pulled me into his old boned body and gave me a hug that felt as though he was giving me all his reserves of energy, bravery and self-assurance. I walked away from the embers of the dying fire with renewed vigour ready for an adventure.

CHAPTER SEVEN
SAYING GOODBYE

I woke the next morning having had a deep and relaxing sleep, I think I had Taliesin to thank for that. The reassuring conversation, warm fire and good food had been just what I needed, and I was resolute in my impeding adventure. The sun was beginning to rise and break through the drifting clouds, as I watched from my window, my first thought was for Heligan. I realised I would be leaving her behind, my only friend, the one I loved. I crept down the wooden ladder as quietly as possible, my mother slept downstairs by the fire and the shrine to Gallam. She was still asleep as I slipped out of the door and made my way to Heligan's family hut.

Her mother told me she was in her cell preparing for the Feast of Dawn. Her cell was just a private hut built by her father so that Heligan could prepare and meditate for ceremonies and rituals, so proud were her parents of her achievement of becoming a Harridan.

She was a much-loved only child, a miracle they did not expect, and I wondered if they knew the risk she was taking because of Ethan.

I walked toward the small hut and knocked. Heligan came rushing to the door and pulled me roughly inside. She was breathing fast, had wet cheeks from crying and a look of panic was set on her face.

"Raykal," she breathed heavily. "Thank God it's you - I'm so scared - they are going to come for me I know it - someone has seen me and Ethan together. Someone has told on us! The Harridans will not forgive me... I don't know what to do!"

My first reaction was to shout, "It wasn't me!" But then she would know that I had been watching and I didn't want her to think badly of me. It was gratifying that in that moment, she seemed to need me. Me, little Raykal the Unnamed, the annoying follower.

The terror in her eyes said it all and we both knew that life on the wrong side of the Harridans could be petrifying and lonely, you only had to look at my mother. This was also a best-case scenario, the worst was torture and maybe even life as a Skim. I shuddered, hugged Heligan and tried to sound as grown up and as reliable as she needed me to be.

"We could hide you - what about at Tarnade castle?"

"It's too close to home, they will track me down." I knew she was right, they had magic on their side.
I thought for a moment, then realised the only way to help her was to take her with me.

"I'm going to find my brother - you could come with me - get away from Tarnade altogether?"

She came closer to me, she looked beautiful with her green eyes glistening with tears. She sobbed on my shoulder in a torrent and I could feel the wetness penetrate my shirt.

"Yes, yes!" She sounded so scared. "When do you leave? I'll go find Ethan."

"Oh, I didn't..." She didn't hear me and I found myself whispering, "...mean Ethan could come." She grabbed her cloak and ran in the direction of Ethan's home. I was left with my childish dreams of being her hero and of just the two of us travelling together as companions unhindered by others.

So, by the next morning I had two travelling companions and my mother felt happier that I wasn't on my own 'for a while yet.' It was time to say goodbye, we had our packs, with a change of clothes and food. My mother was calm, but her eyes were reacting wildly, searching for hidden mysteries and maybe she did know something of the problems I would face along the way. She touched my cheek and her hand was deathly cold. I held it with my own, spreading the warmth I had to her. We smiled at each other, we didn't need words really, but she told me to "Take care," and I nodded. As I turned away from her, I didn't look back, it would have been too heart breaking. Instead I reached in my pocket and felt my talisman stone, it was warm and smooth and comforting, as it always was, and I thought how grateful I was to have a mother and a home to come back to.

I was to meet Ethan and Heligan at the castle. Heligan had spent the night there, cold and scared that the Harridans would come looking. She had told her parents that she was at a Harridan meeting, they always accepted that. I was worried about what her mother and father would say and do, she had told them nothing, afraid that they may be questioned by the Harridans and if they knew nothing, they could say nothing. She also felt she was letting them down; it must be a terrific pressure to be a miracle child and hold all your parents' hopes, dreams and expectations.

Ethan had an aunt in a village about fifty miles away on the border, the plan was to go there. I wasn't sure if I trusted Ethan and I know he didn't trust me but maybe it was a time to get to know him better? My mother always told me not to make judgements about people, as you didn't know what else had influenced them. I believe that I am open minded and unbiased in general, however when it came to love, and I did love Heligan, I burned with jealousy. I didn't want to share.

As I approached the castle, all was silent, but as I entered the familiar, battered entrance, I could see the two of them huddled together behind what used to be an internal wall. They were deep in conversation, their heads so close it was as if they were conjoined twins. That familiar tweak of jealousy coursed through my veins, but I ignored it as best I could.

"Hi you two," I whispered.

Ethan jumped up, pulling a dagger from his belt, the stress was palpable on his face. His eyes looked like those of an eagle swooping down on its prey.

Realising it was me, Ethan bowed his head "Sorry, you can't be too careful... Heligan's worried."

"Best we move out of here and get going." I looked directly at him, I didn't want him to see that I was equally as worried and fearful as he was.

We gathered up their things and marched out of the castle grounds. Like many possible armies before us, we quickly marched past the Harridan Ritual Glade, looking behind us constantly and expecting an attack with every crack of a stick under our feet or movement of a creature or a tweet of a bird in the hedgerows.

Tarnade's sparse forest opened up to fields of corn and vast plains; a wild, lonely, all-consuming wilderness. I felt a sense of freedom and adventure but also a sense of unimaginable loneliness.

I shivered at the possibilities.

The lushness of the grass turned into mottled greys as its expanse travelled on into the distance. The haunting majestic landscape was enhanced by pinks and purples of the muted sunrise and a coating of shimmering mist floated, wispy and hollow. I stepped forward with my hopes high but I was full of uncertainties.

We walked together in silence at the beginning, as there was still a certain amount of tension, but as we crossed the Tarnade border into Travis, a small county where they grew hops and produced ale. I think Heligan relaxed slightly, thinking she had escaped from the Harridan's revenge, I still had my doubts. I remembered what they did to my mother when she fell in love with my father. After the torture, they made it a condition that she stayed in Tarnade for surveillance - she knew too much to let her go. They have left her in relative peace; however, she didn't try and leave Tarnade with Harridan secrets – Heligan, on the other hand, had.

The day was sweet with sunshine but with a cooling breeze which meant that walking was easy and we made good mileage despite being weighed down by our backpacks full of food.

I hadn't really spoken to Ethan much, but I was dreading it, I couldn't hide my dislike of him and I think he had issues with the past and the connections between our families. We stopped briefly for some food, but all felt we needed to get as many miles as possible between us and Tarnade. I walked ahead as I held the map and the compass. This also gave me some space from their amorous exchanges.

The evening started to draw in and Ethan suggested we stop and make camp, there was a small group of trees on the plain and we decided to stay there. I felt excited about sleeping under the stars. Heligan was nervous and whilst myself and Ethan collected some fire wood, she put a protection spell around the camp using stones and some animal bones she had in her pocket. Once a Harridan always a Harridan, she cast a circle and whispered incantations calling on the Gods of Nature to protect us. I watched her whilst I built a fire, feeling her nerves and fear deep in my own self. Ethan went off with his dagger and returned with a rabbit, which he skinned and tied to a large stick and we let it roast over the newly formed flames. We had bread, cheese and apples from home in our backpacks but I think our mouths watered with the thought of meat in our bellies. We had walked most of the day and we were hungry.

We sat in silence around the fire, just staring into the flames and listening out for wolves, Meads and other creatures – we were used to being cosy in a cottage, warm in our beds so this was very different and we were all deep in thought about what we had left behind. I remembered my mother's frail hand in mine, as we said goodbye and her sunken cheeks. I prayed that she would look after herself until we could all be reunited as a family.

"What are you thinking about Raykal?" Heligan broke my train of thought and brought me back to the fire with a thud. She must have been studying me.

"Just about my mother," I replied.

"Yes, it's sad to leave the people we love." She sighed, changing the direction of her gaze to Ethan, he in turn smiled at her and I looked away, it still hurt.

"But also good to be with people we love," Ethan replied and I felt the nausea rise within me.

Heligan saw my look and carried on talking, "You haven't spoken much you two, I'd like you to be friends. You both mean so much to me." There was a sense of pleading in her look. Ethan and I looked at each other and then looked away.

"Ethan?" Heligan said, taking his hand and pulling it gently but with meaning.

"It's difficult Heligan," he spoke low, as if he didn't want me to hear but, I could hear every word. "Her mother... she killed my mother." I reeled in disbelief that he had actually spoken the lie out loud.

"That's a strong accusation Ethan." Heligan spoke in my defence, she looked up worryingly in my direction.

"Nonetheless it's true, Elena tended my mother when she gave birth to me. My father said my mother died because she wouldn't follow the ways of the Harridan, that she wanted to do things differently."

I felt indignant and protective of my mother's reputation; my mother had attended many births and people trusted her. I knew Ethan's father to be bitter and old before his time and my mother had mentioned the story, when she told me to stay away from their house.

"Ethan - I'm sure she did her best." Heligan placated him but fidgeted uncomfortably.

I felt my blood boil with frustration, that I had probably carried with me since seeing them together. It overwhelmed me.

"No Heligan, don't talk about things you know nothing about!" I shouted, "Ethan, it was your own father's fault. My mother wanted to get you out quicker. She was struggling, she had been in labour for hours, her blood pressure was high, and you were in a breach position. A cut would've meant the birth could have been over quicker, but your father refused to have her body 'mutilated.' It's against Harridan law to have anything but a natural birth. But my mother had done this procedure before, she knew what she was doing. Your father insisted - it was *HE* that killed your mother ... his own wife. Ethan you were also lucky to survive. Your father has lived with that terrible guilt and to try and lighten his load he's turned to blame others. It's just not fair! My mother is a good midwife but she has been spurned and rejected and battered with stones for being Vermin, for making a mistake for love - just as you two have done!"

I felt my lungs rasp as I remembered to breathe. I tried to hold back the tears, startling myself with my outburst. I must have carried so much anger and frustration inside of me all those years. So many times, my mother and I lowered our heads, take abuse, accept the stone throwing hatred from those who were really no better than us.

The two of them just stared at me. Heligan, with a look of admiration that I had never seen in her face before and Ethan with a look of disbelief. I had, after all, just attacked his father and accused him of killing his mother. I felt I had to say something.

"I'm sorry Ethan but that is the truth and I won't hear lies told about my mother." I sounded defiant.

He put his head down and looked dejected, "My father loved my mother ... he couldn't have ... just no."

I felt his pain and hurt, "I'm sorry, I could have said it better, but it is the truth."

"Don't speak to me Raykal, why should I listen to a 14-year-old girl... go away! I can't stand it anymore." I knew then that I had got to him, or the truth had anyway. Heligan looked from me to him - torn. She knew I would only tell the truth, she knew my mother was a good person and a good midwife. After all, Heligan was a miracle baby, thanks to the herbal drinks my mother concocted for her's to drink.

At the same time, she could see that Ethan was upset by the attack on his family and so she put her arm around him but looked up at me with a mix of respect and accusation. There was nothing I could do, I refused to backdown. I got up, fed the fire with some more wood to keep it going through the night and then climbed into my sleeping blanket and turned over.

I heard Ethan move away, mumbling something about needing some space. Heligan came over to me and placed one of her cool hands on my forehead and pushed my hair back.

"I am always so jealous of your black hair Raykal." She sighed, I didn't move. "I know you told the truth about your mother and I'm proud of you for speaking up.

She continued to stroke my forehead gently and it seemed to dispel my mood - some magic spell no doubt. I moved round and grabbed her wrist, "I love you!" I blurted it out like a poison, if it stayed inside me any longer, it would probably kill me. She laughed a little hysterically.

"I said I love you Heligan – I always have and I always will."

It was a last-ditch attempt and I let go of her wrist. Her face was a mix of defeat, fear and sadness. "I know," she said slowly. "I didn't want to be a Harridan, Raykal, but my parents, they were, well … insistent. It offered us so much security for the future and I think they wanted to protect me from relationships and their pitfalls. The trouble is that if someone makes you do something you don't want to and that goes against the way you naturally are, it's going to go wrong." I was shocked, she always seemed to love the Harridan experience, but when so much faith and expectation is put upon you, maybe you just try to make the best of it. Love, however, was in Heligan's soul and had won out in the end.

Her eyes exuded grief as I gazed into them and realised this was the most sense, I had ever heard her utter.

We both smiled as she turned away. "I thank you for loving me." She said.

CHAPTER EIGHT
THE CHASE

The next day we carried on with our journey, the grasses were longer now and they turned into fields of corn, not yet ripe, but with long strands of strength. Heligan seemed more at ease now that we were away from the borders of Tarnade and the stress of whether the Harridans were going to strike had diminished - or so she thought.

It was turning into a good day, the sun was evident but not ablaze which made walking easier. There was a breeze coming from the west, it blew us forward instead of thwarting our progress. The three of us had reached some sort of equilibrium after last night's honesty. Breakfast had been awkward, but nothing more was said on the subject of my mother, or Ethan's mother and we all worked together to clear the camp, douse the fire and move on as quickly.

As we walked, I strode ahead, a little embarrassed by Heligan knowing of my feelings for her, realising I was going to have to accept that the two of them were in love with each other. You don't anger the Harridans and risk their wrath for nothing.

'Why is there always a warning from nature when a catastrophe is about to happen?'

A large cloud covered the sun like a blanket and the wind stilled. I looked up and saw a flock of birds fly with conviction away from the trees and hedgerows to our left, squawking madly. I looked around at Heligan and Ethan to see if they had noticed, but they seemed to be oblivious, walking side by side at their normal dreamy pace.

Without warning, thunder seemed to be upon us, but it wasn't the thunder of a storm, it was the thunder of hooves from ghost horses. Horses that were transparent so that their skeletons were visible, their muscles pounded out the strength in their legs and could be seen stretching and pulling their limbs. Their faces were white bone, with eyes like torches seeking out some sort of solace. Were they alive? I wasn't sure but I knew magic was involved as their manes were like lightning bolts shattered into pieces. Riding the first ghost horse was Ammute herself. Kicking her steed on, her hair and cloak intermingled to create a battle flag behind her. They were travelling fast. Following were the other Harridans riding in hierarchical order, as always. I knew they wouldn't let it go, one of their own kind turning her back on all they stood for and then trying to escape their clutches without punishment. If they let Heligan go it would undermine all their authority in Tarnade. The thundering hooves made Heligan and Ethan wake up from their stupor and run. Heligan's face was ablaze with terror and Ethan too was petrified

"Raykal!" Heligan cried out. "They have come for me!"

"Run, Heli, run!" Was all I could manage to say, as I turned on my heels. My brain was working overtime – 'how could we escape the powerful magic of the Harridans? Surely, we were doomed?'

Then I remembered my quest, I had to find Gallam for my mother's sake. I wasn't going to be dragged back to Tarnade. Heligan too had done nothing wrong but fall in love, 'why should she be hunted down like some animal?' I felt that rage, that hidden, repressed rage rising inside me again.

The galloping, underworld creatures were gaining ground on us mere mortals running for our lives. I turned back and saw the horse's heads were now dragons' heads; the metal bits between their jaws pulled them open and sheets of brazen flames came roaring out. Our only hope was to get into the wooded area ahead as there would be more places to hide than the open fields. The heads of the Harridan riders transformed into serpents with eyes like slits of gold, tallons sharpened, clawed teeth and a hissing, slithering tongue darting in and out, hungry for consuming flesh. 'Was this real or my imagination?' I couldn't decide, I didn't have time to decide. Ethan was pulling Heligan now, he was faster, stronger, but they were quite a bit behind me and I questioned whether I should return to them and help pull Heligan but I was too afraid.

"We need to get to the trees!" I shouted back breathlessly and gestured in the right direction. I saw

Ethan nod and so turned around to push forward. I thought my lungs were going to ignite; they burned as I ran with all the speed I could manage. The trees were getting closer but the sound of echoing hooves were also closing in. I really couldn't afford to look back again, I just had to hope Ethan and Heligan were right behind me now. I passed the first tree, I touched it with my hand, steadying myself. I kept running, looking for a place to hide. An old oak was on my left side and something, or someone, told me to go around its huge trunk to the other side where I found a whole in the wood – big enough for me to hide in. Sure enough my sweaty and tired body just fitted into the crooked space. I reached around the trunk and poked my head out; my breath rasping, short of oxygen, it was hard to focus. I was overwhelmed with exhaustion and fear, but I needed to tell Heligan and Ethan where I was and direct them to another tree. I looked toward the forest opening and almost fainted with terror at what I saw.

Heligan's beautiful long russet curls were on fire, the red of her hair could no longer be seen as fire engulfed her head, the flames whipped around her ears like a licking tongue. Ethan threw her on to the floor and covered her in his tunic, starving the hungry flames. Heligan lay there with a blackened face and a singed scalp bereft of hair. I wanted to run back, but I couldn't move, self-preservation had kicked in. A Harridan was placing chains around Ethan's hands and feet and another was bending down over Heligan and placing some sort of salve on to her empty head. She didn't move.

"Move, Heligan, move," I whispered to myself, "Please be alive... please."

I felt for the stone deep in my pocket and I rubbed my fingers over it, offering it a secret prayer, knowing there was no magic in the stone except for the comfort it gave me. I peeked again through the branch and saw them lift Heligan on to a cart that was at the back of the line of Harridans. Her eyes were open, but they had a dead, distant look, as if all her will to live had been taken away. Now the magic had achieved all that was needed, the horses had returned to normal. I felt so selfish wrapped in the safety of the oak bark when only a few yards away, my friends were being dragged back to Tarnade in disgrace.

I saw Ammute climb back on to her tan horse and look up towards me and the forest, I backed myself deeper into the trunk and held my breath as I heard the clatter of hooves coming closer. I knew their power, I knew what they could do. They wouldn't want Ethan or Heligan dead, they would be made an example of back home, then they would probably become Skims. I stifled a sob, not sure if it was for myself or the doomed pair. The breeze picked up and the leaves rustled around me. The horse halted the other side of my tree, it was so close I could hear the snorting of its nostrils. I held my breathe, but my heart was shaking in my chest and my limbs were numb.

"Raykal Unnamed I know you are there... listen to me... you are no loss to us... like father like child ... know this... you will not be allowed to return to Tarnade. You are an outcast and will never benefit from our order or protection again. You tried to help one of our own escape, knowing that it went against the laws. You showed no desire to gain a name ... you will never see your mother again." Her voice rang clear without hesitation and without a hint of cruelty, but instead filled with revulsion, as if I was nothing. I didn't move from my place and she turned her horse around and galloped back to the group. I relaxed my body and allowed myself to peek around the trunk to see Ammute re-join the others. The Harridans were back on their horses.

Ethan and Heligan were chained up in the cart. I thought I could see Ethan's face searching for me and I believe I saw a glint of accusation. He probably saw me as weak and feeble, as I didn't go to their aid or fight to free them. I could imagine him whispering to himself, "That's just like Raykal and her kind - the nameless are a waste of time." A strong irrepressible anger burned through my body. 'Why was I a nobody in their eyes?' I am somebody and yes, I hadn't saved them, but I saved myself! Defiant selfishness. I picked up a stone from the forest floor and threw it hard, pouring all my hatred and anger for the Harridans and Ethan's judgement into it. Obviously, it never reached its target. They were long gone, the abductor with her hostages, self-satisfied that the order of things would be restored once they were back in Tarnade.

I realised that I was completely alone, with just the sounds of the forest for company. The birds had returned and they tweeted their messages incessantly and I just cried, sobs bursting from my chest with tears running down in waves. I cried for Heligan and what she would now face, but I cried more for myself and the friendship I had lost. I cried because I would never be allowed back into my home. I cried for my mother; 'would I ever see her again?' I couldn't believe it. The sobs went on and on, until I ran out of energy and I was spent.

The night had started to draw in and the air became cold. I began to collect some firewood for warmth and protection. It didn't take long to build a fire and it gave me purpose. I took my bedding roll out of my backpack and pulled out the rest of the bread and cheese. I choked on the bread, it was dry and hard, I just didn't have the hunger there to tackle it.

A wolf howled and a faint smell of must and lavender filled the air, but I knew the fire would protect me. I remembered Taliesin and the meal we shared over a fire just a few nights ago. I looked deep into the blazing fire in front of me, grateful for its warmth. As I stared at the curling and twisting flames, Taliesin's face seemed to form in them and the sizzling of the embers turned into his voice...

"You are not alone child; you are never truly alone ... be brave and you will find a way to carry on your quest."

I curled up tightly into my bedding, in the hollow of the tree that had protected me thus far and was for now my only company. I slept despite my fear, my anger and my sadness because I had simply exhausted myself.

CHAPTER NINE
BROKK

I awoke at first light, covered in dew with the fire smoking and smouldering. I felt hungry enough to eat, but I had left my bread and cheese out and some forest creature had long since finished them off. I packed up, there was nothing for it but to move forward. My way back had been cut off, there was no return. I stamped out what was left of the fire, took a last look over my shoulder and moved on further into the woods.

I had the map and compass that my mother had given me along with a list of possible battlefields, but because of the Harridan riders I had mistaken a turn and I didn't really know how to get back.

The sun was high in the sky and I was grateful for the shade of the trees, but I knew I couldn't stay in the forest as I needed to find the path over the fields. However, as well as the shade, I wanted to feel the protection of the trees as I still carried the fear of the Harridans coming back for me. I didn't know what Ethan was telling them or indeed Heligan - they may have wanted to save their own skin and tell lies about me. I was growing paranoid.

I knew I was weak from hunger and I'd eaten some red berries that were on the bushes, they smelled and tasted sweet, so I guessed they couldn't be poison.

It wasn't until mid-afternoon when I realised that I really was lost and there did not seem to be a way out of this woodland. My stomach started churning. I felt dizzy and lightheaded - I guessed it must have been the berries. I grasped the corky bark of the nearest tree to steady myself as I doubled over to throw up bitter, yellow bile. The forest floor was becoming boggier and I hoped this meant fresh water was nearby. In my urgency to find the water source I tripped and dropped the compass, it disappeared under the mud, sucked in like a greedy child slurping its soup. I fought the mud, trying to grab the compass back, but each time my fingers found it, it slipped out of my grasp again. In the end, the mud claimed it as its own.

As I dug deeper into the woodland the trees seemed to close around me. The thud of hooves followed me and mimicked the thumping of my temples. These were ghost hooves and my mind imagined an army hunting me down. I threaded my way through the mangled undergrowth, roots reached out to trip me up and some tendrils criss-crossed together to capture me in a net. Dodging and weaving my way through that maze of entrapment made me lose the will to continue. I was dazed and confused.

I rested against a tree and closed my eyes, when I opened them again a mist had formed around me. It wasn't a cold air mist, but warm and musty like moulding fruit. Thinking again, it wasn't fruit it was sweet and syrupy lavender. I breathed in deeply and my body relaxed, my eye lids felt heavy and I closed them again. I began to drift and dream, dancing over the forest floor... floating... smiling to myself and then I remembered my mother talking to me and I forced my eyes open, like she told me, and there it was. A Mead!

I was surprised as it wasn't dusk, the light was soft, but it was still afternoon; 'they don't appear till dusk,' I thought to myself.

He looked at me through curious half-moon eyes, full of questions, his pupils tinted yellow like butter. His head tipped to one side and all I could think of was that if I reached out to touch him surely my hand would go straight through him. His lips were bent in what couldn't be called a smile but more of a question. He touched my forehead and it was the softest touch, like a feather had landed on your face.

"Human?" He asked. His voice was gentle, almost a whisper.

"Yes." I replied. I hadn't moved an inch and he hadn't stopped staring. There was an awkward silence as we studied each other. I noticed his eyes were circled with dark shadows, which added a sadness to his face. This was balanced by the sparks of vitality and hope in the yellow pupils. His hair consisted of a crown of white feathers and white ringlets which ran down past two pointed ears. There was a tattoo on his forehead, a group of lines in a pattern that had no meaning to me. High cheek bones, a strong jaw and those full crooked lips completed the face in front of me.

For once in my life I did not feel afraid. I had grown up being warned away from these creatures, they weren't to be trusted, but I didn't feel under threat at this moment. I was as curious as he was, having only seen a glimpse of one when my mother and I were out mushroom picking late one night in the woods. He shook his headdress of white feathers.

"Hello, my name is Raykal." I smiled tentatively, still unsure of his reaction.

"Brokk," his voice reminded me of twilight, a magical time of transformation. He offered nothing else but obviously found me fascinating, as he moved his hand over my face.

"I'm lost… I dropped my compass… can you help me?" I asked hesitantly, as he pulled his almost transparent hand away from my face.

"Possibly, but in return you can tell me about your way of life. We have lived beside you for so long, but no one likes us. I am curious about humans. no one can know that I have helped you. Meads and humans don't get on!" His tone was still airy and tinkling but his face was serious.

"I understand," I carried on with my plea. "it's important that I find my way to Navisian and the battle fields as my mother is ill and my brother is missing so I have to find him. Can you guide me through the forest? I will tell you anything you want to know."

"What do you eat?" he replied. Communication might be more difficult than I thought.

"Meat, vegetables, fruit, milk, cheese…" My mind was thinking fast, I hoped he was going to help me. The questions came thick and fast, some random such as; "How do you wash?" Others deep and soul searching; "What are your views on war?" But they were relentless. I tried to answer each as honestly as I could before reminding him, that I needed help.

"I will take you home!" Brokk announced producing a stick, which he implied was a weapon that could give me great pain if he wanted it to. He proceeded to prod and poke me with it pushing me along, I found it all quite rude.

"Can you stop? What are we doing?" But he seemed not to understand and continued with the questions whilst we were moving. With every answer his eyes seemed to flicker with either enjoyment or satisfaction.

The forest became denser still, the trees wider at the base and taller through the branches that spread over us like a canopy. They whispered and hissed gently with the wind as if telling of our arrival. Branches, leaves and thicket became impenetrable and we had to bend and contort our bodies to navigate it. Brokk was very adept at moving through the forest; as a novice, I tripped and bashed and gained more bruises.

Brokk stopped suddenly saying, "We are here."

I looked around, nothing screamed settlement or home to me, nothing was moving, no sounds except for the trees. The light was fading gently, but in this thick undergrowth it already seemed like dusk.

That moment when the two worlds, reality and strangeness, collide. A time, my mother said, when it was easier to talk to the dead and receive messages from the fire, as the divide between worlds was unveiled at twilight. Thinking of my mother brought a twinge of longing and I wanted in that moment to see her face and touch her hand. We waited and waited as the light became darkness.

"Where are they?" I asked impatiently.

"Wait," was all he said in reply. The wind seemed to drop, and all was peaceful, with an undertone of eerie silence.

I felt a heightened awareness and a strong lavender mustiness in my nostrils. My eyes darted about resting on each tree trunk with both expectation and dread. Nothing seemed to have changed, but there was no sense of movement or sound or any speculation of any presence of anything – human or animal.

Just a strong smell of herbs and magic. The aroma put me into a semi-trance, and I became mesmerised by the trees as changed shape, stretching and forming odd shapes. I wondered if I was demented, maybe the berries and no sleep had seeped into my brain and stolen my powers of reason? The elasticated bark popped as creatures broke out of the tree, flittered around in mist and landed. The overwhelming smell of lavender enveloped me.

A crowd soon formed around me. These creatures were smaller than me, so I looked down on them, their features were like that of Brokk's very slight and delicate, all with those incredible dark shadowed half-moon eyes. What stood out the most about their eyes were the sparkling yellow pupils that gave them an intensity, as if they were looking deep into your soul. They all had ears with pointed tips and curls of hair tumbled either side. Many of them had so many feathers in their hair that it was hard to tell where the feathers stopped, and the hair began. This gave them an unkempt look, but their clothes were a contradiction to this as the furs and animal skins were sewn skilfully and neatly. The most noticeable thing about their bodies was how pale they were - almost translucent, but I suppose I already knew that they could morph into a mist and so this made sense.

They came closer, their heads on one side as they were studying me, and their fine boned fingers explored my hair, my clothes, my face. I felt embarrassed and automatically covered my face with my hands.

"Stop!" The voice was gruff and crotchety. I looked between my fingers to see a face aged with wrinkles that made his eyes even sadder but also wiser. Instead of feathers he had what looked like an old ram's skull on his head, the horns curling round to the long pieces of white hair coming out messily from underneath. He looked neither friendly nor cruel.

"Brokk why have you brought a human into our midst? You know how we feel about interaction with humans!" He looked sternly at Brokk, who winced, and his words were met by a cascade of yeses from the crowd and mumbles of agreement. I guessed this man was a leader.

"She was lost... alone... I wanted to know about her life... is this wrong?" There was some muffled agreement from the crowd for Brokk's words, but not as many as for the Chiefs.

"Brokk but what are we supposed to do with her now?" This was a new and aggressive voice, a young Mead with shaggy black hair mixed with blue feathers. He had an arrogance about him, it was in his dark eyebrows and thin lips. I noticed he carried a large slingshot attached to his belt. He had a tattoo on his forehead, but he wasn't close enough for me to see which pattern it was.

"Aiston, I thought everyone would be interested in her and we could find out more of their ways... the humans that is." Brokk protested.

"You're stupid Brokk, she could be a spy, planted in the forest for us to find, they were active yesterday. I saw them near the woodland opening!" There was a collective sharp intake of breath then lots of tutting and sighing at Aiston's accusations.

"I'm not..." I tried to speak up for myself, but I was shouted down.

"Tie her up!"

"Dump her!"

"Burn her!"

"We don't want human interference!"

"Get her out of here!"

The older Mead, with the creases on his face and cloudy yellow eyes that had faded with time, lifted up his hand and shouted,

"Stop!" Again. He continued, "Aiston you are too rash to accuse and Brokk you are too free with your choices. I know the younger ones among us are curious about them as they have had little dealings with humankind, but we must all remember that we cannot trust them." He looked sternly in my direction, but not aggressively.

"What do you think we should do with her father?" Aiston spoke, coming forward from his position at the back of the crowd. Although the talk was about me, I was largely being ignored. Aiston took one look at me, seemed to sneer and then turned his back. "I can take her back to the forest opening; she can find her way back to wherever she came from?"

"No, we will wait till morning, the hunting party will be back, and we can ask Breena to connect with the nature spirits who will guide us." The elder Mead spoke authoritatively and with conviction, as if the conversation was over. The crowd was quiet.

"She can't just wander the camp." said Aiston sneering at me again from under his dark brows. I wondered what his problem was.

"I will watch her Alffrigg." Brokk interrupted, he spoke directly to the older man whilst ignoring Aiston, his eyes wide with hope. "She is my… responsibility after all."

It was then that the crowd came alive again with the chants of, "Tie her up… tie her up… tie her up."

I squirmed slightly and tried to open my mouth again to speak but there really was no point - they didn't want to hear from me, that was certain. Brokk looked over and I thought I saw an apology in his eyes. The arguments about what to do with me went on into the night and I ended up tied to a pole in the centre of the clearing.

Brokk came and knelt in front of me, he looked at me with that sideways look. I asked him for some water, I was parched and he brought me some in a hand-crafted cup made of wood and a bowl of food which looked like mushrooms and herbs in a thin broth; it tasted heavenly and I ate it with gusto as I hadn't realised how hungry I was.

"They think you are a spy sent by the Harridans." His head moved from side to side as if he was trying to ascertain if I was indeed a spy, "I don't think you are."

"I'm not a spy," I assured him, "I hate the Harridans… they took the friends I was travelling with." I told him the story of what had happened to Heligan and Ethan.

He listened intensely, as if he was not just hearing me but experiencing my fear.

"Yes, I see but you must understand the Harridans hate us Meads."

"Why?"

"They hate us because we know where to find the Eve Stone mineral – we know where the mines are - we deciphered the Hieroglyphs years ago and now we protect the mines. If they were disturbed the whole eco system would be harmed." That was a lot of information to take in. This was what the Harridan's spent their time searching for and what I had always wanted to know.

"Why the Eve Stone?" I think he realised from my question that I wasn't a spy, as I looked totally lost and shocked.

"The Eve minerals can give humans eternal life… obviously, that is what they want."

"Right, that explains a lot for me." I had so much to think about, the cogs in my mind were clicking frantically and the weights and pulleys of my brain were rebalancing. At the mention of a stone I immediately thought about my own little gratitude stone and I wanted to run my fingers over its smoothness but being tied up, that was impossible.

"What does the, or an, Eve Stone look like?" I asked wondering.

"It has hues of green and yellow, it can produce flashes of colour when it is turned under sunlight."

"I'm not sure but I think I have an Eve Stone Brokk - reach into my pocket." He reached in and pulled the stone out. I felt a pang of uneasiness that someone else was touching it. Brokk took the stone and rolled it in his palm and then clenched it in his fist.

"Why are you doing that?"

"To feel the heat. A true Eve Stone gives off a rejuvenating heat… this is definitely Eve Stone. Where did you find it?"

"At Tarnade Castle, near my home - I found it on the ground I liked the colours and the smoothness." Sadness ebbed as I missed my hideout, it seemed a long way off and a long time since I had felt those rough castle stones under my fingertips.

"It will bring you luck, look after it Raykal." He placed it carefully back into my pocket and I was sure I could feel the warmth of it.

Brokk got up to leave, I didn't want him to go and leave me tied up on this pole all night. The Meads had all disappeared to collect food and go about their night-time business and it felt lonely.

"They said a human had visited you before - who was that?" I hoped to stop him with my question.

"Two in fact but I was very young, I didn't get to ask any questions. I like to ask questions and find out things." I laughed to myself at the number of questions he had fitted into our short journey.

"What were they like? What were they called?" I asked.

"Looks as though you like asking questions too Raykal!"
We both smiled at that; it was the first time he had smiled,
and his eyes crinkled slightly. To hear this odd being say
my name out loud, sent shivers along my skin.

"One has visited several times - his name is Taliesin, he
is an old man, who knows much about herb lore and
creates healing brews. He comes here to collect the wild
garlic and Reishi mushrooms, which we have in
abundance and also to ask advice of the elders."

"I know Taliesin" I said wistfully, longing for his
presence and the smell of home. "He said to me before I
left that he counted you all as friends and that I might
learn from you myself. Obviously, I didn't know at the
time I was going to end up here but maybe he did?"
I realised that Taliesin did know; he had known that I was
going to meet the Meads and I smiled to myself.

"Yes, he is a good and clever man - the only human we
trust, I think … The other man stumbled on our camp,
he was a vagrant from Tarnade, he was being chased by
the Harridans. I think he had taken something, something
they wanted or needed? It's all pretty vague to me, I was
young, but I remember he had red hair and was large and
he told stories of the humans, which I and Dain really
appreciated."

"Dain?" He hadn't mentioned him before.

"Ah Dain is my friend, he is our entertainer, he collects
stories and retells them. We grew up together, he plays the
Reedle so well. Wait till you hear! You will meet him

tomorrow, he is on the hunting party led by Alfrigg's partner, Alva." Brokk was talking excitedly now and it was good to see another side to him from the rather serious and awkward creature who found me.

I thought, 'Yes, they look different, but really, we have more in common than we think.'

"A Reedle?" I asked, I had no idea what he was talking about.

Brokk laughed and it sounded like a cascading stream. "It will all become clear tomorrow," he said. "Don't worry and sleep well."

With that he vanished into vapour and into whichever tree was his home.

I was left with my thoughts. I now knew what the Harridans were looking for and why. Taliesin knew all the time I would end up here, and yes, there was obviously a lot I could learn from these creatures, even I knew that. However, I knew that I must not forget about why I was on this journey. I thought for the first time about Gallam, maybe lost and alone like I was, injured and crying in pain somewhere and my mother wasting away in our cottage, not knowing.

I had to remember my quest.

CHAPTER TEN
LIFE WITH THE MEADS

I slept well. Brokk gave me some sweet-smelling straw and a lavender scented blanket, which may have helped. Although I was tied up and the prisoner of a group of creatures I had been told all my life to hate and fear, I felt very at ease and protected within their clearing. I remember thinking last night that I felt more secure and at home here with strangers, who so far had not been at all friendly, than I did in my own hometown or in the school with the Skims, whom our society trusted and respected.

It all seemed very wrong to me. My thoughts were disturbed by singing coming towards the clearing. I was obviously exposed in the open, so was the first to see the return of the hunting party.

It was led by a beautiful Mead woman; it was her red hair that I first noticed, plaited and tied with blue feathers.

The colour of it made me think of Heligan, but this woman's forehead was tattooed.

She also had a noticeable scar over her left eye, which looked like an animal scratch. It did not deter from her beauty which spoke of fierceness and strength.

Directly behind her was another woman, she looked completely different from the general look of the Meads, she had no feathers, but her hair was wisps of golds and greens, whilst the front of her head was crowned by small antlers. Her skin was so transparent it seemed to glow, green veins covered her shoulders, the same glow emanated from her eyes where the yellow pupils were enormous in size. I presumed she was someone special. Both women carried spears.

Next in the party were two Meads supporting a large branch over their shoulders which had rabbits, stoats and hedgehogs hanging from it. Another two Meads had baskets on their heads, both made of reeds, one was completely full of fungi of different shapes and the other smaller basket was full of berries. Finally, from the rear came the singing, the voice was clear and full of joy, it reminded me of the folk singers back home who told old tales of times gone by and brought the past back to life. The voice came from a large muscular Mead with long, brown, owl-feather hair, a beard to match and laughing eyes. As they neared camp the barks of the trees began to stretch like elastic as, with a lot of muttering and excitement the Meads came out to greet the arrivals.

As they approached my post, the beautiful woman stopped and looked directly at me, at first with surprise, but then her piercing eyes darkened to hatred. As I looked up at her in awe, she spat at my feet and screamed a guttural piercing sound, which led to her forcing the spear she held towards my face. I retreated back as far as my rope would let me.

"No, Alva!" The golden woman behind her had grabbed hold of her spear arm and gently made her lower the weapon.

The glowing woman then came towards me with her outstretched hand and without touching my face she seemed to scan it. At the same time, she closed her eyes and with her other hand touched the small polished stone that was placed in the centre of her forehead below her antler headdress. The whole Mead village waited in silence and I dare not move. A minute passed but it seemed like a lifetime, my life hung in the balance and it all depended on this one Mead woman's decision. I could see Alva's menacing spear out of the corner of my eye - it was ready to strike. At last she took a sharp intake of breath, and then exhaled a heavy sigh. She opened her eyes and they glistened at me, reminding me of my mother's eyes when she read the flames.

These eyes were like yellow flames themselves.

"Alva you must leave her alone, this girl is safe, she is clean, she means no harm at all." It was then that she smiled at me, her smile was a glow of warmth. "My name is Breena, Spiritual Healer to the Meads, and you are?" She lowered her hand to reach out to mine and I automatically reached out to hers. As we touched a feeling of wellbeing, hope and comfort wrapped me in a blanket.

"Raykal," I answered smiling. I was in total awe of this lady I had just met. I was released from my chains, but obviously I couldn't sleep within the trees as the Meads could, I was not able to vaporise into mist, so the inside of the trees would remain a mystery to me. They set me up in a stable style building, used to keep the animals; goats for milk and chickens for eggs. There was plenty of soft straw and it was warm. I know I should have moved on, but with the loss of Heligan I felt that I needed others with me and, I had an intuition that these fairy folks could teach me things that would be useful.

My friendship with Brokk grew every day, he had another mountain of questions about humankind and I asked questions in return. Some Meads were friendlier than others. They were all wary, but they all seemed to trust Breena and accepted me as harmless and not a threat to their way of life. Brokk took me out walking to see their territory and it was truly beautiful: forests that were untouched and wild with flowers and grasses I had never seen before. Brokk said it was because Tarnade was polluted by the Harridans and so many plants did not grow there anymore.

There were fast flowing streams with water so cold and clean that it refreshed your thirst in seconds. Small brooks with ghostly slivers of water that glistened in the sun. Beautiful waterfalls flowed and cascaded over the rocky outcrops. Everything seemed idyllic, a playground where the Meads bathed, rested and worshipped the water as the giver and preserver of life in a joyful way with Reedles and singing. A Reedle was like a flute but deeper and reedier, of course they were made from reeds, so had a vibrating element, like when you put grass between your thumbs and blow.

The Meads seemed to worship everything about nature, not in a religious way as the Harridans did in their own rituals, but in a joyful way, that encompassed everyone. They didn't just worship nature from afar, as if it was some mystical god, but instead used nature for everything; their clothes, their food, their instruments and hunting weapons. Their philosophy being that it's there to use, but to use completely, not wasted and of course, replaced.

What became evident, after just a couple of days was how equal everyone was. There was no leader as such, although the older Meads were respected for knowing more, because of their accrued wisdom. Weekly meetings were held to discuss things, which meant lots of shouting, flying opinions and rudeness but no one took umbrage; it was all sorted in the end with a majority and everyone moved on with little resentment. There didn't seem to be any rules except for mutual respect and dignity. It was a surprise to see that segregation and hierarchy simply did not exist. The Meads found the Harridans both amusing and disturbing and this is why they could be seen visiting and playing tricks on the inhabitants of Tarnade, as well as doing their job to protect the Eve Stone Mine, which involved spying on Harridan rituals and rites.

Brokk told me that Alva had been captured once by a human and had been tortured. She had been incapable of escape as the Meads are unable to turn to vapour until dusk, hence the scar over her eye, knife marks on her arms and rope scars on her wrists. It had traumatised her so much that she now had a loathing of all humans.

'No wonder she tried to kill me when she first saw me!'

I thought of the Skims and the fact that they are torturers too but were also once normal people who opposed the Harridans and were tortured themselves. It all seemed cruel and stupid - a circle of hate.

'Maybe, torture is something people do to others when they don't understand them?'

I discovered each Mead had a tattoo on their neck, forehead or arm that depicted their sacred tree, determined by when they were born and the traits of their personality.

They received this 'ogham' at a coming of age ceremony which took place at a secret location, I wasn't to know about. I respected this and so didn't pry. I was also surprised to learn that the Meads did not marry; they stayed with a partner for as long as they wanted to and then moved on, there was no loss of respect. Their children were not treated any differently.

When I told Brokk that I was an 'Unnamed' and daughter of a 'Vermin', he had no idea what I meant. He just said, "But your name is Raykal."

"I know," I tried to explain, "But I have no surname - no last name."

"Neither do I. I am Brokk, surely one name is enough?" We both laughed about this, it seemed to make perfect sense.

Aiston was still a problem, he seemed to resent my presence. He was the son of Alva and Alffrigg, so I suspect he hated the humans for what they had done to his mother. There was also jealousy between him and Brokk; he resented that Brokk had found me and not him.

Brokk told me that Aiston thought he was better than everyone else and bullied many of the weaker Meads. He also respected strength and forthrightness and was an excellent hunter and protector so there was obviously another side to him.

Maybe a hard shell to crack? Whatever his problem was, he always looked at me with disdain, he never attempted to talk to me and so I left him alone.

CHAPTER ELEVEN
RAYKAL AND THE STAG

I was told that if I wanted a share of the food then I would have to do my bit in attaining the food and indeed cooking it. I was quite prepared to do this, I had hunted before with snares and slingshots, but never with a bow and arrow, as the Unnamed were not allowed to carry these sorts of weapons.

Alva was leading another hunting expedition that morning, just a daytime expedition to get some rabbits, berries, nuts and herbs. There were five of us. Alva was leading, as she was a seasoned hunter, Dain the singer and a quiet girl called Elga. Elga was Alva's daughter with Alffrig; she had an amazing head of white dove feathers. Dain and Elga shared many a sideward glance at each other and I wondered if there was something between them. Brokk and I brought up the rear. We stopped at a grove of cherry trees planted by the Meads themselves. They shared with the birds of course, but there was plenty to go around. The red shiny nuggets of juicy cherries were picked and basketed within half an hour and we moved on.

The party split up as we reached denser forest and Alva went off on her own, always a loner who preferred her own company and her own ways, she went down to the river's edge to look for stoats and mink.

Dain and Elga, were given baskets to find berries, nuts or herbs and Brokk and I were given sacks and the slingshot and charged with the task of finding rabbits. Although the Meads were mainly vegetarian, they did eat meat, but they insisted the whole of the animal was used. For its meat first, but then also its coat for clothes and bedding and its bones for medicine - they believed there was no point killing a living creature unless there was a purpose to it. The Meads were not greedy, they didn't stockpile animal meat and they refused to use traps that might maim or torture an animal rather than kill it. They preferred to kill using a simple slingshot and they were adept at using them - taught from a young age.

I was not allowed to have a slingshot, I was not considered good enough, although I had been told to watch and learn. Brokk knew the rabbits liked to eat wild garlic so he had led me to a part of the forest where the floor was matted with the plant. We were in a clearing surrounded by small trees and bushes. It was one of those sun dappled days where the light through the forest made the place seem dreamlike and hazy. We began to crawl on our elbows, so as not to scare our intended prey. I could hear a woodpecker drilling the bark in the distance. As we crawled into the garlic mixed with grass, the heavy scent filled our noses and bees and butterflies fluttered around us. A rabbit dashed past, its nose twitching. Brokk prepared himself but the little creature scurried away. It was then that I noticed a movement ahead of me, I reached out to touch Brokk as a warning for a rabbit but missed his arm completely. It wasn't a rabbit.

As I looked ahead, I could see the wise and superior face of a stag; it didn't move and just stood silently watching me. The birds continued to twitter and the bees to buzz and the breeze to catch the grass and make it rustle. For that moment there was just me, Raykal the nameless and this stunning creature. Like a carved statue, but with eyes full of memories, knowledge and life and I was mesmerised by it. He raised his regal head and snorted loudly, then bowed down and tapped his foreleg on the ground as if in greeting. In that moment there was no one else in the world but us and I breathed in the intensity of the moment.

Suddenly out of nowhere I heard the bracken crunch. I looked up to my left and there was a human face staring out from the bush. It was a shock to see a human, I had only been here a few days, but I had been immersed in the culture of the Meads and had forgotten about the other folks out there.

Surprisingly, now I didn't see them as allies or friends, but as the enemy. This unforgiving feeling towards them was fuelled by the bow and arrow I saw perched in his hands pointing at the deer. My heart wrenched, as I knew he was going to target the stag. I looked around me to see if Brokk had noticed, but he was busy spying on a rabbit nibbling nearby. I didn't know what to do, I didn't want to put the Meads in danger. If the humans saw them, they could harm them or try to capture them. I know the hatred and mistrust that they felt toward the creatures, because once I would have probably felt it myself. But also, I didn't want this majestic stag, with whom I had made a deep spiritual connection, to be harmed. I didn't have time to think any more and I jumped up from my squatted position, ran toward the deer and hollered at the top of my lungs. The stag took one more look at me, there was a madness in both our eyes. It bolted.

The arrow left the bow and I felt its sharp tip puncture the skin of my leg. I screamed even louder and fell forward, feeling the warm garlicky ground come up to meet me. As my head came to rest, I could see a sideways view of the bush as it rustled and the human, whoever it was, fled without a backward glance. I grimaced in agony but smiled inside in triumph. My stag had escaped.

I must have lost consciousness. When I woke, everyone was gathered around me and through a mist of pain I could see Brokk mopping my brow with fresh spring water, which was cold and must have brought me back to life. I could feel someone ripping my trousers.

"It's ok Raykal, Alva has made a compress of sphagnum moss for the wound and Elga is making you a compound of garlic and nettle to ease the discomfort - you will be ok."

I nodded my thanks and then rolled my eyes back into my head as a wave of agony overwhelmed me.

"I told you Brokk, she's nothing but trouble, a liability." It was Alva's voice breaking through the mist, as she held my head and forced me to drink some vile liquid, I choked.

"Drink it!" She ordered.

"But she did it to save a stag, I saw it bolt, she did it to save our sacred animal Alva, it shows great valour and daring, surely you can see that?" Brokk was defending me and I must admit, even in my delicate state, I felt a sense of pride.

I slipped into a semi-conscious state and slept and woke simultaneously. I heard snippets of conversation, "We have to move her!" and "Get her back to the village!"

These were intermingled with the face of my stag, snorting and thudding its hooves, with terror in its eyes, an arrow flying, the stag tumbling, and a human perched precariously on top of the stag's limp body, looking victorious. Someone held my hand. I cried. 'Did I save the stag? Did he die?' I was carried, I don't know how.

"Will she be ok?" Someone asked.

"Is my Stag ok?" I asked. My mother came to me in a fog and tried to speak to me, but I couldn't hear her, she was faint and unclear. Ammute approached, holding something out to me… it was Heligan's head, the auburn hair was recognisable, but the features were that of a Skim. I screamed.

When I awoke from my nightmares, I was buried in a fresh pile of straw in my little shed and Breena and Alva were sitting next to me. I smiled limply, Breena smiled back and Alva sighed; I was not sure if it was with impatience or relief.

"Welcome back Raykal, you have had a fever but you have come through - just relax and we will look after you." Breena touched my forehead with her cool hand she flipped my fringe to one side and for a moment, it reminded me of Heligan and how she had touched me the night before the Harridans came for her.

I found myself crying, without struggle or effort. Tears just trickled out of my eyes, down my cheeks and Alva wiped them away silently while Breena told me to sleep. I slept soundly, without the haunting dreams that had filled my fever. I woke up hungry, Brokk was there smiling down at me with a bowl of something hot in his hands. When he put it into my mouth, it tasted heavenly, although he said it was only a pumpkin broth. I propped myself up on my elbows and ate it all, I winced with pain when Breena placed a new herb poultice on my wound, but she said it looked as though it was healing.

Aiston appeared in the doorway, arms folded with his usual look of disdain and contempt, but as he came closer his eyes had a softness I had never seen in them before. "How are you?" He asked tentatively.

"Much better." I replied.

"Everyone is worried about you, we have all taken it in turns to sit by your side - we all want to say thank you for what you did and against your own kind!" He cast his dark eyes downward as if in deference – I couldn't believe it, 'was this the same Aiston?'

"I just didn't want the animal to get hurt, I had no idea the stag had special significance to your people but I had looked that animal in the eye, our souls had connected, and I couldn't let it die, it was that simple."

"What you did was brave and selfless, you put me and others to shame. You were prepared to die for the sake of another. We, as Meads, value this trait highly. We didn't think many humans possessed it. Maybe you Raykal, have taught us something."

"Thank you Aiston." I touched his arm, and he in turn touched my hand. He carried on speaking, passion in his sparkling eyes, "It's the fact that you saved a stag, the most important animal to us. It lives immersed in nature and drinks from the stream just as we do. It protects its territory and has antlers that look like the arms of trees. An ancient story tells of a stag helping to protect the first Meads to populate Eveiss from the arrows of the humans. That stag was white and twice the size of a normal stag, it befriended the Meads and they rode on its back and explored the forests and glens finally finding the place where we are now; Stags Hollow. The stag has always been a symbol of change, regrowth and renewal of life, it too changes with the seasons, as does all nature and the stag helped us to find our home. So, for that reason, we will always protect the stag and all of the deer family here." I had never seen him so animated and expressive; he was usually moody and sullen. I realised that these creatures were complex and multifaceted and not the simple, malevolent fairy folk of the Harridan lies. Finally, Aiston and I had reached an understanding.

My leg continued to improve and in a matter of days I was up and about with a crutch that Dain had made for me. The Meads in general had changed their demeanour towards me; they smiled more, they weren't so suspicious. I had grown in their esteem - it was a glorious time for me, feeling confident and respected. I wanted to learn more and more about these fairy folks and immerse myself in their ways. But as my strength came back so did my guilt and the need to fulfil my quest to find my brother.

CHAPTER TWELVE
THE EVE STONE MINES

Early the next morning, Brokk came to my stable door, he was agitated, his eyes darting about as if he was afraid someone might see us.

"Raykal, I want to take you somewhere, but we have to leave now, before anyone wakes!" He hissed.

I was still half asleep and dozy enough to be unsure if I wanted to leave my cosy straw manger.

"Come on Raykal… it will be worth the effort, I promise."

"Ok, ok, I'm coming." I dragged myself out of bed and put on my jerkin, I no longer needed a crutch or a stick, although I still limped slightly, but my leg was healed and I felt strong.

"Why are you so restless Brokk?"

"It's Alva and Breena, they've told me not to take you out of the village, yet. But you seem strong to me and I feel I have to take you there." He hesitated, "before you go?"

His words hurt a little, but yes, I did have to leave at some point.

"Let's go then!" I said. All was quiet as we left the enclosure and we walked through the woodlands, in the same direction as when we went hunting, but this time we went past the garlic grasses and deeper into the thicket.

Brokk led the way, at quite a fast pace, but he checked constantly to make sure I was just behind him. It was unusual because Brokk normally liked to talk, he was never short of questions but he seemed set on this mission. There was little room to walk together anyway, as the brambles became thicker, we were forced to walk in single file.

We spent an hour walking deeper into the bracken which was thick and thorny, as if it was protecting something precious. The rain had set in today, with droplets like fine hair that irritated and covered every part of you. It was as though we were walking through a mist. Our progress was slow but steady, bent like predators to ease our way through the undergrowth. As in a jungle, the ivy clung to the boughs of trees like twisted ropes. Broken branches and warped boughs made faces of bears and dragons appear on the trunks. Brokk stopped at a Rowan tree, bent and twisted in shape. Bright red berries clung to its branches, we had eaten many of these with the Meads and I presumed he was going to pick some to take back. I saw him place his forehead and hands on to the bark for a single moment of concentration. I knew it was his tree and he was paying homage to it.

Around me some of the branches of the trees were so thin, through lack of light, that they tangled together to create covered walkways, that we strode under. The drizzly grey day was occasionally broken by the golden tones of an early sun, it dappled on the stream in shadowy lines as trees embraced and enfolded each other. We moved on. Piles of bracken and twigs meant we had to jump and twist our bodies to get around them; this was a good work out for my well-rested leg.

Green sprouting bluebells, not yet broken out of their buds, made a carpet for us to crawl on. Finally, we slowed down and came across blocks of stones piled one on top of another, it could, at one time, have been a wall. Now it was beyond my recognition, reclaimed by moss and ivy and spots of lichen. Having moved some of the creeping greenery, I could see it was a wall on top of a wall, the different shades of bricks and stones highlighting the many years the structure had been there. The damp and shady conditions meant the algae and liverwort had spread slowly over an area of cobbled walkway, that lay beneath the shade of the stones. At the end of the cobbles there was a small opening, a mouth, encased in old grey wood scaffolding and was covered with curtained hanging ivy vines that, unless you were looking directly at, you would never know it was there.

"This is the mine that contains the mineral, the Eve Stone." Announced Brokk proudly, "I'm showing you as a sign of how much I trust you."

"The one the Harridans want?" I reached automatically into my pocket to feel for my own stone, afraid the Harridans had come in the night and taken it. It was there, safe and sound.

"It's well-hidden." Brokk continued. "You cannot get here unless you are led to it by one of us." I thought about the protective vines and thorns we had wound our way between, under and over, I would never be able to remember the way here or indeed, the way back.

"Can we go inside?" I wasn't sure I wanted to, but felt I needed to.

"We can go in, but you must be careful, it is unsafe in places."

"Maybe just a look?" I replied hesitantly, ever since I was small, I had never liked closed in spaces; spaces where you felt trapped or couldn't get out from, I was much happier outside.

"Hold my hand." As usual Brokk had sensed my feelings and offered me security.

We walked down the cobbles and toward the opening, we pushed the ivy-like vine to one side and entered the darkness. There was no light, so we had to give ourselves time for our eyes to adjust. We walked in further, there was a dank, clammy atmosphere. Puddles of water lay under our feet. The walls of the tunnel were jet black and shiny like polished coal. It wasn't cold though, in fact, there was a heat that emanated through the walls themselves. We carried on carefully through the entrance tunnel, I was still holding Brokk's hand and was concentrating on dodging the puddles, then he stopped in front of a huge inner cavern. The sides were carved out in slatted patterns and interspersed with green and faded yellow seams that looked like arteries and veins radiating out from the rock. Light was seeping in as the place was lit dimly, but it was enough to give this mighty cavern a magical glow.

I inhaled with awe.

"It's beautiful isn't it?" Brokk spoke softly but his voice echoed, giving it a tinkling effect like the little bells on the feet of Mead dancers.

"Yes," was all I could say, other words escaped me.

"This mine and the Eve Stone are so important to us and to your people too. If the Eve Stone is mined and demolished then the delicate ecosystem we live in will also be destroyed. Our little world will slowly diminish. We must protect it at all costs." It was the most serious I had ever seen Brokk look or sound since our first meeting.

"I understand Brokk, I really do. The Harridan's must not be able to get hold of this mine." I hoped with all my heart that the mazes, books and maps they scrutinised and ritualised over would always be too complex for them to decipher. However, I also knew their magic, their power and I felt sick with the knowledge that it was possible they could find it. A sense of panic rose up inside me; how was it protected, apart from it being difficult to find and surrounded by thorns and bracken? Would that stop them? I doubted so.

"We have our own style of magic Raykal," he had read my thoughts again. "We use our collective energies to place an invisible defence around the mine, only those Meads who created the protective shield can break it." He gave me one of his cheeky lopsided smiles. So, the Meads were not magical individually, but collectively they could produce enough magical power to protect the mine. I didn't really comprehend what the collective energy was, I was still thinking about the Eve Stone mineral itself and studying the beautiful iridescence of the golden-green seams.

"How can this mineral give immortality Brokk?"

"It contains the same enzyme as the evergreen trees, they never change colour or seem to age. If the mineral is ground up and consumed in water or food it will give humans a long life and a youthful appearance."

"But what's the point in living forever, if the world you live in is destroyed?"

"Exactly Raykal. However, the Harridans don't care about the planet, they will bleed it dry. They probably think they can save it with their magic, but that will only make it false and fake; their streams will not have fresh water, their trees will be made of concrete and their sky will be a slave-built dome." Brokk spat out the words, with a bitterness and venom that I hadn't seen previously in any of the Meads, least of all in him.

"I feel afraid Brokk, that this will happen." I also realised that there were more pressing issues and problems, than gaining a name in Tarnade.

"We should go." Brokk brought himself back from the brink of hatred. "I just thought it was important for you to see it, it's a privilege and an acknowledgement of how much we trust you, very few humans have seen the mine or indeed the Eve Stone."

I took one last look at the glowing rockface and couldn't help reaching out to touch it, one more time, and feel its warming energy. Then I reached into my pocket and pulled out my own Eve Stone. What a privilege to see the place this special stone was born. I kissed its warmth and put it back.

We walked out of the mine and started making our way back through the tangle of branches and undergrowth.

It was then that I heard, what I at first thought was thunder, but then realised it was horses' hooves and I had heard that sound before...

"Brokk! It's the Harridans, they are close by, what shall we do?" I was thrown back to that moment on the road, with Ethan and Heligan, when I first heard the thunder and turned to see the dragon headed horses of the Harridans flying towards us. Brokk ran back towards the mine and placed his hand on the trunk of a Rowan tree, well known for its properties of protection. I knew now he was resetting the protection spell. We then dropped low to the forest floor and buried ourselves behind a nearby Holly tree. We automatically made our breathing shallow and stilled our wildly beating pulses, something the Meads did often and that I had learned from them. The forest us was thick and matted with vegetation, deep roots of trees escaped the earth like great claws of mythical beasts and the canopy was overhung with drooping branches and cascading leaves. The chaos made it an impenetrable place, defended by its inhospitable aura. It was indeed well protected, but my fear was that the Harridans were getting ever closer, no doubt one day they would discover the mine and would the Meads' collective magic be strong enough to repel them? I shuddered. I caught a glimpse of a chestnut mare and a flare of a emerald cloak, as they made their way through the maze of roots, bushes and undergrowth less than three hundred yards from us. They did not stop or pause but they knew they were close, their noses were in the air smelling the mines' presence and sensing what the Eve Stone could bring them. The horses trotted on and the green cloaks flapped in the breeze. Time stood still as we hoped with all our might, holding our breath, that they wouldn't see the hidden opening. One of the Harridans stopped, looked intensely at the map in her hand running her hand over a set of figures and hieroglyphs on another piece. I remembered watching them from the castle, as I had many times, immersed in their rituals of magic and discovery.

I realised 'the answer' that Heligan constantly referred to was what they were searching for... the Eve Stone minerals were hidden here and protected by the Meads, the very creatures we were told to distrust and avoid. No one knew back home, and this knowledge made me feel an immense panic, as well as an overwhelming sadness that this revelation would mean some sort of loss to me.

CHAPTER THIRTEEN
THE TREE OGHAM

That night I slept restlessly, the stags majestic head still appeared before me but this time he was shaking his head and his antlers broke off and turned to dust as the autumn leaves fell around him. I felt a longing inside myself and a deep sense of sadness, which I hadn't felt since Heligan was taken. The stag turned his back on me and I watched him disappear into the shimmering woodlands behind, which were lit with the pure gold that only autumn can bring. I was thinking to myself that it was only early summer and not autumn. Next my mother appeared, she walked towards me out of the golden sun streaming into the forest. She wore the purple tunics of the Harridans and although she moved her lips, I could not hear what she was trying to say. I could, however, see the concern in her eyes and she raised her arm and pointed in the direction of the forest path, already walked by the stag. There in the place of the stag stood a group of Harridans, a map in their hands, staring ahead and pointing at me.

The gesture told me in no uncertain terms that I needed to move on, I had been here too long.

I woke from my dream in a sweat and was full of frustration and anxiety wondering what I should do, I knew what I had to do.

I couldn't ignore the message. I had to get on with my quest. I turned in the hay and went back to sleep, I would make the most of tomorrow with my friends and then tell them that evening that I had to move on.

It had indeed been a good day, full of making baskets, foraging and laughter. It was tinged with sadness for me, but I don't think any of the Meads guessed at my internal grief, but as the day went on, I found it harder to hide. The sun was beginning to set when Brokk found me, my head in my hands.

"What's wrong with you?" He asked in his usual easy-going manner. I looked up into the face I had grown to love and trust. It was such an open face, constantly questioning, painted and preened. I knew it so well now, what had once been unusual and slightly scary was now comforting. 'How could I leave it behind?'

"You have to go, don't you?" I laughed at this perceptive comment, I had forgotten for a moment how insightful and observant these creatures were.

"Yes Brokk, I have been here too long. My mother came to me in a dream last night, to remind me that I have a job to do - I must find my brother. I have dallied here too long, only because I have fallen in love with you all and have enjoyed learning all about your wonderful culture."

Brokk looked dejected, but then a change of countenance came over him.

"I have come to take you somewhere and it's even more important now you have told me you're leaving." He reached out a hand to me and pulled me to my feet. He didn't let go but held my gaze and walked backwards. I didn't question where we were going or why, such was my trust in him.

The sun had said her final farewell and the redness of the sky was turning to a dull grey. This was the Meads' favourite time of day, when they felt the most themselves, most free and they hovered about as mist and body with the heavy scent of lavender filling the air. As we left the village enclosure and moved silently into the trees, I noticed there were no Meads about either floating as mist or sitting together singing, or playing the Reedle, sharpening their hunting tools or arguing about some important matters as they usually did at sunset. I smiled to myself remembering the wonderful evenings spent in this place. 'But where were the Meads?' I was going to ask Brokk, yet I was concentrating on where we were going and where I was putting my feet, my eyes were not as good as Brokk's. We walked for maybe ten minutes in silence. Brokk leading me by the hand, he walked fast paced and my eyes were peeled to the ground, watching out for roots. He stopped suddenly and I looked up.

What I saw in front of me was simply... beautiful.

There was an old tree, a Willow. Its twisted branches were covered in clear glass lanterns, orbs of pure silver light that matched the moon. The tree's complex maze of roots, ancient and gnarled, were exposed and under them ran a cascading waterfall. The water pushed its way through the wooden crevasses, glistening in the light given off from the globes above. It was all very magical around the grove and all standing staring at the tree was the whole Mead community; the smell of lavender permeated the air.

"Welcome to our Tree of Divinity, Raykal." Said Brokk, staring directly at me. "Tonight, you will receive your tree ogham and become an honorary Mead." At these words the Meads all started clapping and stamping their feet and I just stood wide eyed and overwhelmed with emotion. Brokk led me past all my friends; Dain winked, Aiston saluted, Alffrigg nodded and Alva touched my shoulder in muted affection. That small gesture meant the world to me. Breena was waiting for us at the end of the tree roots. The waterfall was playing its own music, it felt like calmness and excitement at the same time.

"Welcome Raykal... we have brought you here to share one of our nature rituals and bestow on you a tree ogham tattoo, but first you must connect with the Willow Mother who will decide your ogham. Are you willing to accept this honour Raykal?" I knew it was a great honour, they were a secret, closed society who mistrusted humans and they had taken me in and taught me so much.

"I will," my voice was croaky and was overpowered by the trickling water, so I took a deep breath.

"Thank you." I said loudly and deliberately. They clapped and cheered again.

"Now silence," said Breena. "Let us all clasp hands and let Raykal communicate with the Willow Mother herself." A mass movement took place as all the Meads grasped their neighbours' hands and Brokk took one of mine, Breena the other. "Close your eyes Raykal and think of all that you believe in and want for yourself," Breena whispered softly.

I closed my eyes tight and listened intently to the cascading water and the kiss of the breeze, I asked myself silently what I wanted, 'what did I believe in?' I knew I wanted my brother and mother to be safe, but I also thought of my father and realised that I wanted to know where he was, who he was, if that was possible. However, the strongest emotion was to defend these lovely creatures and preserve their way of life, ultimately preserve and hold in high esteem what they did and protect all nature, the ecosystem and the Eve Stone.

"Open your eyes Raykal," Breena whispered again to me. As I did, I saw a face appear in the wizened trunk of the tree. It was a kind, wise old face completely made of bark, the husk of hair pulled back into a bun, a high forehead, a strong nose and warming smile. The head was cradled in between two branches that looked like arms and hands holding it in place. The calm countenance didn't change as she opened her eyelids to reveal two black currants. There was a sense of expectation in the air substantiated by sighs from all those around. Her mouth opened. "Welcome," she gently spoke, her voice was like the singing of the waterfall, like when your mother touches your forehead when you're ill, like a whisper of the lightest breeze on your ear - pure magic.

"I am the Mother Willow; the white lady of the moon. I am here to give you your tree ogham, now place your palm against my trunk and I will read your very soul Raykal of no name."

Breena, took my hand and placed it on the rough trunk and, just as with the castle walls and I felt the pulse of life and the weight of history. The Meads themselves started humming a low pulsating hum, as if they were of one body. The Willow Mother closed her eyes again and all went silent, just the running water of the waterfall, in the darkness, with the slight shimmer of a full moon breaking through the cloud.

Time moved on and the clouds cleared to reveal the whole of the moon and when I looked closely, the face in the moon was like the face on the sacred tree. The silence was broken as everyone's eyes opened once again.

"Raykal you are an Oak through and through, in your heart and soul. The Oak symbolises: durability, constancy, purity, strength and survival. You are an honest, brave and generous spirit with the heart of an adventurer. You may not believe this yourself, but it is there deep inside you

Raykal. I think you are connecting with your true self and this tattoo along with protection from your spiritual tree will enlighten you further. Good luck my dear." The eyes stared deep into mine one last time and I felt renewed.

Breena stepped forward, brushed my dark fringe to one side and painted the simple ogham of the Oak on my forehead. Dain played his Reedle and the Meads sang a haunting folk song about the gift of trees, the value of the air we breathe and the patterns of the moon and stars. I felt the reed needle cut gently into my skin and the drip of the inky substance make its mark. I felt a surge of confidence and wellbeing that I had never felt before. Breena wiped away the excess ink and my own blood with a bundle of moss. It was then that the Meads started coming forward to the tree and tied coloured pieces of cloth to the branches. As each one tied the cloth, they uttered some inaudible words and then, smiling at me, walked away, some waving back to the village. "What are they doing Breena?" I asked.

"They are placing wishes on to the tree for your good health and safety on your journey and when you return each knot of cloth will be untied and a gift left for the Willow who has kept you safe - we care about you Raykal." She kissed my forehead, where her artwork stood for all time and then she turned and followed the others back. Only I and Brokk remained. Breena's words struck a chord and I realised that they all had known I was going to leave, probably before I did. I looked at Brokk and he looked at me "You knew I was going before I told you, didn't you?"

"Yes - it was inevitable - you have something you need to do." He nodded knowingly.

"I am going to miss you all so much, but especially you Brokk," I had to swallow hard as I felt something stick in my throat and I think it was the knowledge that he wasn't going to be with me anymore. "You have been a good friend to me."

"There is no need to miss me Raykal," his demeanour changed from sadness to a smile. "For I am coming with you on your quest!" He announced, so pleased with himself. I couldn't believe it.

"You are prepared to leave everything and put yourself at risk for me?"

"I have always been adventurous and inquisitive - I am always the one that wanders too far or takes a risk. That's how I found you and that's why I have the ogham of the Rowan tree. My people know what I am and accept me, as we accept all of our individual traits, they are happy for me to accompany you and it is ... my greatest wish." His eyes were full of pride.

"Thank you so much Brokk, it will be a pleasure to have you as my companion and with you by my side I will not be so scared of what I have to face." I meant what I said, having him by my side would make a difference, I had not discovered my bravery yet but Brokk was steadfast and supportive.

"We leave at first light!" He raised his hand into the air as a sort of salute and started to stride back to the village like some commanding soldier and I laughed and followed him, feeling renewed with hope and vigour.

CHAPTER FOURTEEN
NAVISIAN

Saying goodbye was wretched, I was surprised by how much I had connected with these once perceived strange creatures and now they were more familiar to me than my own family. I was being hugged and patted as much as Brokk as we worked our way through the crowd that had come to see us off. Both of us wore backpacks stuffed with food and medicinal herbs. Hands were shaken vigorously as shouts of encouragement were trumpeted. At the end of the boundary to Eveiss stood Alffrigg and Alva and Aiston. Alffrigg patted my shoulder in a manly reaffirming way, Alva smiled in her usual disarming and distant way and I knew she wished me the best of luck, even though no words crossed her lips. Aiston said he was jealous and wished he was going with us, half hoping for an invitation I think. Only Breena stood in silence.

Grabbing my hand, she pulled me to her so she could whisper in my ear, "Take care of Brokk Raykal, he is in danger as soon as he steps past the boundary, I fear for him, but you can protect him... only you." I reassured her with a smile but felt the weight of responsibility.

I looked at Brokk being blessed by Alffrigg and realised what a sacrifice he could be making for me. But then I remembered, when we were up late talking on many nights, he talked about his quest for knowledge and his lust for adventure and it really was all he wanted to do. He looked so happy and it renewed my own resolve to complete my quest.

Heligan came to mind for a moment. She had been happy to travel with me then as it had meant she could be with the man she loved.

'Where was she now?' I was pulled back into reality by Brokk slapping me on the back as he caught up with me. His wide smile was infectious, and we walked over the protected border and into the forest, as we looked back only once to see those comforting folks waving and cheering excitedly.

It wasn't long before the mass of trees became open fields again as we walked, laughed and made mistakes together. It was so nice to have a companion whom I trusted and now knew so well. We came across few people on our travels, but this was a war-torn land and I think many kept themselves to themselves, untrusting of strangers, and what a pair we would have looked - a young Tarnadian girl, dark and tall, travelling with an unusual creature with feathers for hair. We passed empty battlefields covered with burial mounds and effigies for the dead that reminded us of our purpose. I cautiously checked each one in case my brother's name appeared.

It never did but I wondered if he was alive.

His last letter had said he was deep in Navisian country and so that was where we headed. After two days we started to climb higher on to the cliffs and to see the cool blue and green mass that was the sea. It was a beautiful sight but also one fraught with danger as it meant we had crossed into Navisian country and were now on enemy territory. They were known to be violent and aggressive people who lived by and in the sea and its surrounding salt flats. Sea fishing, shell fishing and eating samphire had made them a strong, if wily, people that were protective of their life and land. They were a traditional, patriarchal society, they thought a country should be controlled by men and not women - hence their issues with Tarnade and the Harridans.

Neither of us had travelled this far north or seen the sea in reality. I had only seen it in an old picture book my mother had handed down. I can remember it was painted blue and green and there were grey rocks and yellow sand. Now I was mesmerized by the constant movement of the sea; as if it was one big mass, it came crashing to the shore and broke up into a thousand pieces of foam. Then it was pulled by some unseen force back out to the distance again. This was repeated and repeated, each wave more mesmerizing than the last one as I looked for changes or differences. Sometimes the wave came further into shore, sometimes it clutched the sand and stones and chewed them up, other times it did a half wave that was stilted by its own weakness. I felt hypnotised as its magnetism pulled me closer towards it and I instinctively moved nearer to the cliff edge. Almost as instinctively, Brokk flung his arm out and pushed me back.

"Be careful Raykal, I have heard of the powers of the sea, its rhythmic motion has sent many an innocent to their death - I too am finding its music hard to resist!"

"I can't take my eyes from it Brokk... it's enthralling."

"Catch your breath, we need to move on." He was right, it was late afternoon and we needed somewhere to camp, a windy cliff face was not the place.

I breathed in the freshness tinged with salt and turned away from the edge towards the fields.

"I have always been that way with water Brokk, if I see water, I have to go into it. Back in Tarnade I enjoyed swimming in rivers and streams and your waterfalls in Eveiss have such magnetism."

"I too feel the same, my mother was connected to water and her tree ogham was a Willow. I don't remember much about her, she died when I was young but I was told that she loved swimming." I put my hand in his and squeezed. He had never mentioned his parents before, it showed how much our trust in each other had developed on our journey. He looked at me with his yellow, halfmoon eyes. I noticed now that their hue changed from bright sunlight yellow when he was happy to the creamy butter they were now when he was sad or reflective. I had grown to love those eyes.

"What happens when your people die Brokk?" I knew I could ask him anything, but when I was in Eveiss I had seen no one die and no funeral and his mention of his mother made me curious.

"We go to mist, we vaporise like we can do every evening but that time we don't come back. Our body disappears, and our energy absorbs into nature." He spoke in a matter-of-fact manner.

"Wow...no body to bury, no funeral? No goodbyes?" I was thinking it was all a little harsh.

"We usually know that we are dying and have time to say goodbye. It is sad, but we go back to nature, the environment which is, after all, our natural home and we leave no imprint on the earth."

We walked down from the cliffs and on to the grey salt marshes, filled with blue clay mud known locally as 'the stew.' The dyes within the iron and potassium deposits create a rich shade of Prussian blue. There had been books written about this place, about its beauty, with its wide blue skies and flat open plains covered with the greens of grass, the purples of heather and the blues of the mud-filled lagoons. I remember seeing a picture of it and reading about it. The place was also associated with legends; people disappeared here, they just seemed to become invisible, with no sign of anything, not even a hat or a weapon left behind. The Harridans called it the black magic of the Navisians and warned you to be on your guard. I didn't trust what they said anymore after meeting

Brokk and the Meads. I was still wary, they were after all our enemy. Brokk, on the other hand was full of curiosity, as usual, his head spun with every bird that flew by or with every blue pool we passed. He loved all nature so much and everything here was amazing to him. The place had an emptiness to it, a silence that was both beautiful and menacing. A loneliness that matched the Navisian's need to keep themselves to themselves.

"It's going to be an amazing sunset tonight," Brokk smiled.

The ground was getting boggy underfoot and we had to be careful where we stepped, my boots were covered in thick gloopy mud and it was hard work to walk on this swampy ground. It was going to be difficult to find somewhere to set up camp and find anything dry to start a fire. We had to get out of the area before sundown.

"We will have to try and move faster if we want to get past this marsh before dark," Brokk broke the silence of the effort we were putting in.

"It's ok for you Brokk, you can turn to vapour and fly over it!" We laughed; it was true but I knew he would never leave me.

"Why are there no paths?" I continued only to find myself squishing and squelching through more mud. I was losing the will to put one foot in front of the other, it was such an effort. I was tired and we had been walking all day for the third day in a row. I noticed that the sun was indeed getting lower and I was getting worried that we would not escape this quagmire.

Brokk was a little way behind me, studying a small yellow plant that was new to him. I felt my foot squelch once more into the mud, only this time, it was impossible to pull out again. I wiggled my foot around; this strategy had worked before. Not this time! My foot went deeper, and the mud closed in around my boot and grabbed my leg. I could feel the coolness of the mud seeping around my skin. I tried to lever with my other free leg, putting all the pressure on it and heaving with all the strength I had left, but to no avail. The monstrous sucking mud swallowed the other foot and soon I was knee deep in that blue tinged sludge.

Panic rose up inside me, "Brokk! Brokk!" I called breathlessly, "can you help?" He looked up and laughed, seeing me now thigh high in muck, it must have been a funny sight, but he didn't realise the seriousness of the situation.

"No, Brokk, I can't move… I can't get out… this stuff is swallowing me!" His face changed from one of fun to one of concern and he started bounding towards me.

"Stop Brokk or you will be swallowed too - be careful." I felt the cold mud ooze on to the skin of my thighs and the more I squirmed and twisted the higher it climbed. Brokk stopped still. He looked for something to help me with, a tree branch, a piece of wood, something I could hold on to and he could pull me out with, but there was nothing. This ground was open, flat and quiet and not the forest he was used to. I started to shiver, with the coldness of the mud's grip or fear.

"Stay as still as possible Raykal. The more you move the more the sinking sand will pull you down." I tried to stop shaking by hugging myself, or was it for comfort?

"I will go and get some help, there's nothing here - throw me your rucksack." I did as he said, and our eyes met: concern with concern. It was then that we heard the rumble of hooves on hard ground. I stiffened as it reminded me of the thunderous hooves of the Harridan's dragon horses. We both turned and saw a small pack of soldiers; the one at the head holding the flag of Navisian, I recognised the boat and the axe, both symbols of the country emblazed in gold on a black background. I presumed they were out-lookers, they spotted us and then changed direction. I was nervous as they were my enemy and I had heard rumours of their aggressive and violent ways. At the same time I needed help to get out of the quagmire I was stuck in. They were dressed in leather jerkins and their hair was long but tied back with some sort of dried reeds into pony-tails that stretched down their backs. The man at the front had a rugged face, scratched and torn by swords and by time. His mouth was set in a grimace, there was nothing kind or welcoming about him and I knew we were in trouble. A few yards from us they dismounted from their horses and drew their swords as they tentatively walked towards us, not through fear but because they knew the landscape and where the boggy ground could give way.

"Who goes there?" The Captain asked.

"Hello, I'm stuck... could you help?" All their faces were close enough to see now and all were battered, bruised and tanned a dirty brown – preserved by the salt and the coastal winds. One of the men laughed heartily when he saw me and my distress, he then spotted Brokk and pointed rudely, "what is this? A pet?"

"Hello I am Brokk a Mead from Eveiss." Brokk reached his hand forward in greeting. He was ignored.

"Ah fairy folk," said one soldier dismissively, "not to be trusted."

"But worth something?" Said an even older man gruffly. It was as though they didn't even acknowledge we were there. The Captain spoke quietly and they all huddled around him. We couldn't hear what they were saying but there was a lot of gesturing and grunting and looking over at us, whilst I was sinking further and further into the mud.

"Are you going to help me?" I cried out.

"Quiet girl!" Was all I got back. They seemed to come to some agreement, as heads nodded in acknowledgement. One of the men, the youngest I could make out, as he had the fewest scars and the freshest beard was sent back to the horses and he returned with a large wreath of rope and some wooden boards. I sighed with relief that they were offering help as the cold mud was almost up to my waist and I was shivering. They placed the boards down on to the mud and then threw the rope end to me.

"Catch girl and tie it around your upper body under your arms." I did as the Captain said, although it took me a while as my fingers were icy and numb and the rope thick and bulky.

"Hurry up girl, we haven't got all day." No kindness or understanding was shown. The other end of the rope was wrapped around the three bulkiest of the men, in a precise military operation that they had obviously had to undertake many times before. They walked backwards and the other three men heaved on the rope and I felt the gloopy mud bubble and burp as it spat me out and I was able to cling to the wooden boards and heave myself out still further.

Brokk was waiting on the boards to make sure I wasn't going to slip back in after all this effort. A rough but welcome blanket was thrown over me as I was picked up and thrown to safety by the Captain. Covered in a black, blue and brown mess of mud, I felt weak and cold and could do nothing but sit and shiver. With Brokk's arm around me I didn't even notice the rope being slipped back over my shoulders, blanket and all, until I was unable to move my arms.

"What are you doing?" Brokk protested. Nothing was said but another rope was thrown around his neck.

"Wait," I objected, "don't treat us like this - what have we done?"

"Shut up girl! Did you think we were saving you to help you out?" The Captain snarled, "we are mercenaries, we fight for the highest bidder and make money where we can - the two of you - a healthy young girl and a fairy folk will make good money for us at a slave market or in the camps."

I protested, "I'm from Tarnade!" But I knew as soon as the words escaped my lips that I shouldn't have said it. 'Was I stupid enough to think I would get prisoner of war rights from a group of mercenaries who had no allegiance to anyone but themselves?'

"Even better." Said the oldest man with the white beard and hair, "an enemy, they will pay a higher price." And with that he sneered and scooped me up onto his horse, mud, rope, blanket and all.

We moved off.

I searched for Brokk and saw him being pulled behind another horse; the rope around his neck being yanked by the Captain.

CHAPTER FIFTEEN
ESCAPE AND RECAPTURE

It wasn't a long journey to the first camp, I stopped shaking as the caked mud and the blanket had warmed me. I hated seeing Brokk treated how he was, running alongside a horse with a rope around his neck. The camp was typical of one set up by soldiers by using a once peaceful village. It was a mix of badly constructed reed and mud huts and animal skin covered tents.

Firstly, the children shrieked, and their shouts brought out their mothers, and then the soldiers. The men we travelled with were obviously well known there as they were greeted, if not as friends, then with an air of respect.

"Tark, you are welcome, have you and your men come to join up on the right side for once?" The soldier that spoke laughed heartily at his joke.

"No Bron, but we do have some goods." I was dropped unceremoniously from the horse and Brokk was led forward by the Captain.

"Interesting..." Bron said lifting up my chin. I looked defiantly through him, trying not to see the hunger in his face.

The children and women moved away from Brokk, they looked uneasy and some were visibly terrified. "What bad luck will he bring?" One soldier shouted as he pulled the remaining children away and hustled the women back to their tents and huts.

"Fairy folk can be an asset surely, especially when sold with a Tarnadian?" Said Tark, a noticeable salesman.

"Place them in the cage whilst we negotiate." Bron let go of my chin aggressively and the men dismounted and walked toward the largest tent, whilst Bron called to the women for ale and food.

They clearly knew nothing about Meads and placed us both in an iron cage with wide thick iron bars. Unaware that we knew we could possibly escape once twilight came and Brokk could become mist and open the cage. We just sat quietly and waited. Curious Navisian's came near to the bars to see us closer. Some tentatively reached their hands in to feel Brokk's skin, half afraid that they would be turned to dust and feeling brave in the process. Others came to spit at me for being 'the enemy'. I was once used to being spat at, but it hadn't happened for quite a while and my confidence had increased by being valued by the Meads, so now it seemed harder to accept that people would do something so disgusting to me. After a while, one woman came several times to stare without speaking or spitting or touching.

"Why do you come and stare at us?" I asked.

"Because you are to be my new sister wife." She answered.

"What do you mean?" I had no idea what she was talking about.

"The council have met and they are giving you as a new wife to my husband. I can't have children and so he needs a wife that can. You are young and healthy and will be able to give him the children he so desires and which I cannot." Her face was downcast and sad, like many of the women we had seen here. She was attractive, maybe thirty years old with plaited brown hair covered by a torque style head band made of a dull metal. Her eyes were like that of a deer, large and brown and at this moment full of tears.

"But I don't want to be someone's bride and I don't want to have children!" I screeched at her. "I need to find my brother... *my brother*!" I rattled the cages iron slats knowing full well they would not move, I could feel the sting of angry tears in my eyes. I hadn't come all this way to end up as a breeding machine for some man I didn't know. I knew how they treated women here in Navisian and I think I would rather have faced the Harridans.

"Ha!" She laughed through her obvious sadness, "forget what you want now girl. You are in Navisian now and you are a girl - you do what you are told." With that she walked away without a backward glance. I looked at Brokk and my body shook with an escaping sob, "I'm scared Brokk."

"Don't worry," he reassured me. "As soon as twilight falls, I can get us out and we will escape, I won't leave you,

you know that!" His yellow eyes sparkled, and he took my hand in his and rubbed its coldness into warmth and we just looked at each other, both knowing there was something deeper than friendship growing between us now.

It was at that moment a group of men marched towards us, official looking men in long garments with semi-armour made of leather, including the chief figure who had touched me before. The guard opened the door of the cage, reached in and pulled me out by my arm. I squealed in pain, his hold was rough and tight, and he didn't let go as he swung me round to face the group. I glanced back at Brokk who was left in the cage - he was holding on to the bars with an expression of anxiety and anger on his face.

The door was shut firmly, and we were separated.

For the first time since Heligan was taken, I felt alone. One man stepped forward, he was about forty, his face haggard and lined with scars. His eyes like little black pits peeped out from long grey hair and a matted beard. He came close, as if he was trying to smell me. I pulled myself back away from him as much as I could but the guard tightened his grip and pulled, I winced and followed. The older man touched my hair and sniffed it, I could smell his breath, he was so close, it smelled like rancid fish, it made me want to retch. His hand moved to my face. "Smooth young skin," he mumbled as he then moved his hand down my neck and on to my body. "No!" I shouted.

The guard who was holding me used his other hand to swipe me around the head, "Shut up girl." He ordered, like a grizzly bear.

"Don't hurt her." I heard Brokk's voice through the muffled fog that now encased my head.

"She will do for me - I hope she is a virgin. She is young, healthy and will bear children unlike Lucien, that useless woman I am bound to... I will take her." He turned away from me and shook the hand of the Chieftain and the other lords who were laughing and patting each other on the shoulder.

"Now to celebrate with a draft of ale my Lords." Said the Chieftain.

"What about me?" My voice was small, but it was clear enough not to be ignored.

"What about you Tarnadian?" Said the Chief, "You are lucky not to die - instead I show my mercy and you will have a chance to serve my Lord Railfan and bear his sons - an honour."

"I don't ..." I didn't have time to finish before another whack of a hand came across my face and pain stifled my words.

"Don't mark her, soldier." Said my husband to be. "I want her to look nice for my wedding night." He laughed and was joined by the other men as I was thrown into the cage again and I felt the comfort of Brokk's arms around me.

They gave us food, but I couldn't eat it, I felt defiled and dirty, it wasn't so much that I had been hit and touched it was the fact that I had been ignored. I had begun to feel worthy and confident in the Mead's world of Eveiss. Now I felt myself going back to that young girl following her mother in the marketplace, or in session with the Skims, just waiting for the abuse to come.

The evening started to draw in. We could just see the Navisian encampment, there was a large fire and lots of drunk shouting, talking and merriment. Women were going back and forth with plates of fish on beds of samphire and drinking vessels splashing with beer. Trudging like servants with their beautiful long plaits and escaping hair flowing in the wind. Maybe their hair was a metaphor for their life, bound up and trapped with parts of them longing to escape. You would never know as they weren't allowed to express their opinion or voice their needs.

Brokk's touch broke my thoughts, he whispered,

"The time is now - I can turn to mist, find the keys and release you."

"Please be careful Brokk." I whispered back.

"I will... don't worry. I have played many a trick on people with their keys." He winked as I reached out to pull his face towards me and kissed him hard on the lips. His lips were soft and full and it tingled. I thought about the times I had wanted to kiss Heligan and now probably never would, but this kiss felt exciting and built on a closeness I had never reached with Heligan.

Brokk pulled away, he looked shocked and I was worried. Had I done the wrong thing?

"I have never been kissed before," but his eyes twinkled gold like stars, his lips smiled at me and all was right with the world as he disappeared into a mist of lavender scent.

It was worse waiting; I would rather have been doing something. My mind worked overtime wondering if he was ok, if he was achieving anything, if he would come back and what I would do if he didn't! Darkness fell and the noise of the evening fell with it, the women stopped serving food and drink. They hid in their tents or went back to clean the huts ready for their husbands' return or to tend to their children. The shouting and music stopped and was replaced by hooting owls, coughing guards and heavy snoring. Sleep evaded me, I listened for every sound, waiting for a warning shout or talk of capture. The stress built up with every minute I was left alone. The brute of a guard walked past, he had a beer in one hand and dice in the other, he sneered at me but didn't even notice Brokk was not there - he had other things on his mind.

His footsteps crunched away towards the collection of guards gathered around an upturned barrel, it was a gambling night for them. At that moment I saw keys moving in the lock and knew it was Brokk. 'Yes!' I breathed deeply, for what seemed like the first time since he had gone. The door of the cage opened slowly, Brokk was controlling its squeaks. I slipped out through the gap, feeling a hand on the small of my back and smelling that musky, but oh how comforting, whiff of lavender.

We tiptoed through the compound, towards the trees. My heart was pounding so loudly, I thought the whole camp would hear it. Brokk rebodied himself and we held hands. Simultaneously, we held our breath at every crack of a stick or crumble of a stone as our feet touched them. The moon was not helpful that night, it hid itself behind the clouds, it did not want to be a witness to our escape. Luckily, Brokk had excellent night vision and led the way. As we reached the edge of the camp, I started to breathe again, I allowed myself to hope we were out of danger. What we weren't expecting were the guards ensconced on the camp boundary; naïve of us really, this was a time of war. 'Why would they leave the camp unguarded all night?' We didn't see them or even sense them, the first I knew was the cold steel of a knife on my neck and a strong, imprisoning arm around my waist and arms. Brokk fell to the ground; knocked unconscious by a club wielding guard. There was nothing I could do but watch. I knew there was no point in screaming, or trying to struggle, I didn't want to die, I was sure of that. The guards' grip was constricting, and the knife was held with conviction, I could already feel a trickle of blood racing down my neck. We had well and truly been recaptured and I reeled at the thought of what they would do to us now.

CHAPTER SIXTEEN
DEATH

They imprisoned Brokk in a glass dome like a sand timer and hung it up by a chain next to my iron cage so that I could see him fading hour by hour. It is a Mead's worst nightmare to be denied oxygen, fresh air and nature. He deteriorated quickly, firstly into a deep depression and then through physical weakness. He stopped trying to communicate with me. His bright yellow eyes turned to a milky white and he seemed to become more transparent with every passing minute. He placed his hands on the glass, I was unsure whether he was unable to stand without leaning or that he was pleading with me to help him.

I didn't know what to do.

I was a prisoner myself and about to be given as a bride to some old Navisian brute. I had nothing in my cage except for a few fish bones left from my last meal. I flung them at the glass and they just bounced off without even causing the slightest splinter. Only by shattering the glass could I save him.

I had to think of something, or I would be married and Brokk would be dead.

It was a cold dawn, you could see your breath on the air and there was no one around apart from a handful of sleepy guards who had been on duty all night.

It was then that I saw the woman approach one of the guards. She had the typical Navisian plaited hair, but she wore less clothing than the other women I had seen. In fact, what she wore was pretty revealing, her cheeks and lips were blushed red. When she approached the guard, she touched his shoulder provocatively and whispered in his ear, which made him laugh and relax. She continued to touch him and flirt outrageously until he took her hand and they both disappeared behind a hut. Here, it seemed sex was the only power women had and so I decided to flirt with my guard. He was an ugly brute to look at and also a violent animal, but just looking at my beautiful dying Brokk I had to do something and quickly. I ripped my top, so that my neck and shoulders were revealed and the very top of my small breasts. I pressed my lips together several times to make the blood rush to them and I slapped my cheeks hoping it would give them a blush. Last of all, I ruffled my hair, it wasn't long, but I could give it a bit of body. I then mustered all my strength, took another look at Brokk who was now slumped down on one side and I called the guard over, "Hey Sir." He threw the shell of whatever he was eating down.

"What?" He spoke gruffly and sneered at me.

"I really need some help Sir." I called him 'sir' hoping it would give the impression that I respected him. I awkwardly shuffled forward to the front of the cage. I put my finger to my lips and played with my hair trying to flirt with my eyes and hoping I didn't give any hint of my innate fear. I could see his eyes registering my bare skin. He looked hungry, although he had just eaten.

He licked his bearded lips and looked around hesitantly, his eyes scanning for onlookers. There was no one taking any notice, everyone was going about their daily business. I had counted on him not bothering to ask many questions and I was right - he asked none. He unlocked the door, I took a deep breath, he pulled me out harshly by my arm. I went to talk, but he put his dirty fingers to his lips and pulled me towards the soldiers' huts. My heart was pumping so hard I thought it would break through my ribs. I hadn't thought this through. 'What do I do now?' I panicked. I could feel a wind rushing in my ears and my surroundings became faded.

I was so numb all I could feel were rough gripping fingers.

He pushed me against the fenced wall behind the huts, so hard my bones vibrated. I had to think quickly. He held me in place with one outstretched arm, so I was pinned and then with the other he started to fumble with the strings of his breeches. I could see the keys rattling on his belt.

'Did they open the cage or the glass dome?' I didn't know! I noticed a knife and a hammer pushed into the leather belt, maybe they would be more useful? I surprised myself at how logically I was thinking. His hand moved from pinning my shoulder, to grasping my neck, as if he was holding up my chin. His grip was tight, the air wheezed in my throat. He had finished with his trousers and now fumbled with mine. Getting annoyed, he grabbed his knife and cut my own belt in two. In his excitement his grip tightened. I saw stars. I managed to rasp out, "Don't mark me - the Lord won't be happy." and he loosened his grip on my neck. I simultaneously grabbed the knife and kicked my legs with all my strength towards his crotch.

I felt myself fall, as he reeled in pain. Automatically he let go of my neck and doubled up, cursing at me. I bounced off the ground and with no time to recover, I stabbed him in the back, over and over until he fell to the floor. He rolled over but I couldn't afford for him to get up. He was larger, stronger and would have overpowered me in a second. I grabbed the hammer and finished the fight.

I had no sympathy or malice as I stepped over his limp body. I flew back to the cage, catching my breath. I fumbled, I had to be quick, the camp was waking. I didn't know if the guard was dead or when he would be discovered.

There was a chain holding up the dome. I tried the keys one after the other and each click of disappointment increased my heart rate. The fifth key clinked into place and I was able to winch down the dome, the chain clanking so loudly it could have been a bell to wake the dead. Where I found the strength, I don't know, I was running on empty but just seemed to keep going. I was in this mess and needed to finish it. Brokk was slumped lifeless. I had to get into the dome. I could see no opening and no lock. I heard a yawn and a stretch behind me and the clank of breakfast pots. I remembered the hammer at my feet, picked it up and struck the glass with every ounce of inner strength I had. It shattered into a million pieces, the sound of it was like an alarm. I heard shouts behind me, I didn't turn to look but grabbed Brokk, threw his now slight transparent figure over my shoulder and ran out of the camp towards the trees.

I avoided the area where we were trapped the previous night. I prayed there were no guards around the camp's borders.

I also knew that if they had been on guard all night, they may well have fallen asleep or more likely in a drunken stupor. I was like a hunted animal aware of everything around me, my senses heightened. I moved stealthily all too aware of the scrambling and panting behind me. My saving grace was that the soldiers were half asleep and sluggish and I was alert, vigilant and had a life to save.

I was worried at how light Brokk was but at that moment in time it was an advantage as he didn't slow me down.

We lost them. My time with the Meads had not only made me strong physically and mentally, but I could find my way instinctively to well covered ground.

I positioned Brokk's light and very weak body against an Oak tree and placed my palms against it; after all it was my tree, I had its ogham. I pleaded to the tree to give Brokk all of its healing energy. I even placed my forehead with its carved pattern against it. This was partly to catch my breath and feel its cooling bark but also to add my energies to Brokk's healing. I bent down over Brokk and touched his forehead, talking to him constantly.

"Brokk, Brokk, we are free." His eyes were closed, his lips clamped. There was no response. He had closed down completely, I hoped it was his way of repairing himself. I looked around me like a terrified rabbit in a lamp light.

'Were we safe?' I doubted that the Navisians would leave it at that, for the sake of their pride they would surely hunt me down . We had to keep moving.

"Please, Brokk, please." There was still no response. I cupped my hand into the nearby stream, taking some over to Brokk, he needed water and nature. I tried to scoop the water into his clamped lips, the touch of the smooth, cool water made his head move from side to side. I frantically pressed the rest of the liquid into his cheeks and forehead. His eyes flashed open briefly and his mouth moved.

I put my ear closer to his lips to hear the words; he said, "Home."

I kissed him gently all over his kind, inquisitive face and with each kiss I reproached myself with guilt that it was my fault that he was there, half dead, and not safe in Eveiss. I held his hand and kissed that too, noticing how papery his skin felt, dry like tissue. I so wanted my kiss to be the kiss of life. "I will get you home Brokk, I promise." I remembered Breena's words, "take care of him Raykal... only you can."

Her words echoed, I then cried, it was as if everything I had just been through was wasted. I had killed a man, albeit a brute, but nonetheless I had taken someone's life. 'If Brokk didn't survive then for what?'

Brokk's hand moved in mine. I looked up to see his eyes were open, but they were dark ghosts and the surrounding skin was opaque.

"Don't cry," he said weakly. "I need to go home Raykal, but I will always be with you on your journey." The tensing of his muscles with every word showed that it pained him to speak.

"Don't talk Brokk, save your energy." I stroked his feathered hair, to calm him but he continued.

"Never be afraid... I will return to mist... we all return to mist when we die." I grabbed his paper-thin hand, "don't talk of death Brokk, you are surrounded by nature here, we are free to breathe and live." I was sobbing uncontrollably, I could no longer feel his hand in mine, I was holding air.

"It's too late Raykal... too late... but I am going home." These were his last words.

He faded into a vapour, like the fog you become trapped in on a misty morning and then it disappeared into nothing; *nothing*.

"Where are you?... Where are you?" I cried, the shock was too great, I couldn't comprehend that he was gone. Then it hit- that feeling, the same as when Heligan had gone, a complete and utter loneliness, confusion and devastation. This time I didn't know whether I could pull myself back from this cliff-face of despair. I touched the ground where Brokk had laid, it was just nothingness. I looked up at the Oak with an accusing face.

"Why didn't you help!" I screamed, pummelling the trunk with my fists until they throbbed and were bleeding and in that moment it was a relief, as if my body was mirroring the pain I had inside. The blood was a physical embodiment of the anger and sadness seeping out of me. I crumpled then, laying in the space once filled by Brokk. I was a shaking, shuddering curled up mess, sobbing my heart out.

"Why? Why do I lose everyone I am close to?" I asked repeatedly. The only answer I received was the rustling of the leaves as the wind picked up.

I must have been there all night. When I opened my sticky, swollen eyes it was light again in the world, but all

I could feel was the darkness inside me. My hands were clenched tight and the knuckles spread with dried blood. I pulled open my fingers and there in my palm was a feather, crushed and wet with sweat but a feather nonetheless. It was a white silky feather from Brokk's hair - I knew it! I also knew it wasn't there last night when I was battering the tree. It gave me hope that Brokk had placed it there, but then why, if he was alive, didn't he stay? That sent me again into my place of anger, despair and loneliness.

I gulped, my throat was dry and my eyes were sore with no liquid left to dispel. I kissed the minced-up feather and place it deep in my pocket along with my stone. I touched its smoothness, only for a second but could not feel grateful. I reached over to the stream and guzzled some water down, I wiped my face with its coolness, I winced as it stung my hands.

However, it was good to feel something, anything.

It was then that I heard the barking and scratching of undergrowth. It was the hounds! They were out looking for me.

For one moment I thought let them catch me and rip me apart. My grief was so great. Then a voice in my head reminded me I had a purpose; to find my brother and this made me move. Fast.

CHAPTER SEVENTEEN
THE CAVE

I needed to get into the stream and run, the hounds would not be able to pick up my scent that way. The stream was stony and uneven, but I was now hardened and determined. I had a mission and that was not to be caught and taken back. I didn't know that I had the strength to run. I had not eaten for hours and the events of the last twenty-four hours had drained me. However, my brain was running on stress and my leg muscles clenched and extended automatically so I followed their lead. Every splash of water over my calves was met by baying hounds followed by shouts of angry men. Everything around me, the trees, the sky the thick grasses were blurred, but at the same time my inner pain made the colours vivid and luminous. The stream became a river and I was able to swim, adding mud to my tired limbs. The mud turned to a sandy mulch and I knew I was approaching the sea. The scenery changed to rocks and grassy outcrops. I knew I would be exposed here if they made it this far.

I stopped for a moment, treading water, breathing hard, I had to think quickly.

I couldn't keep up this momentum, my legs and arms cramped and ached. 'What would the Meads do? What would Brokk do?'

My chest sunk with the mere thought of him, my eyes darted - looking, searching - almost as though I was an amber eyed creature from Eveiss. I espied a collection of rocks with a small opening, it was only visible from open water. I swam towards it, pushing my throbbing limbs forward. Exhausted and running out of whatever was keeping me going, I noticed that although I was still within a river, there was a tidal pull that worked with me and I was grateful. I could now see the vastness of the ocean ahead; I stayed to the right and was swept into the rock opening from the current.

I was thrown on to a sandy bank in the cave that looked much bigger now than when I had first spied it. I looked back out of the opening, every part of my body ached and screamed for rest, but I knew I was not completely safe. The tide could rise and drown me, or my captors knowing I had headed for water, could jump into a boat and still hunt me down. I dragged myself to my feet and stumbled further into the dark interior of the cave with the last dregs of energy I could muster. There was a heady smell of mould, mud and salt.

Enough light entered the cave to enable me to get my bearings. I looked up to see a small granite ledge where, if I lay down, no one would see me.

'Could I get up there?' There was no question, I had to. My body wanted to argue fiercely with my brain, my bones creaked, my muscles moaned as I started to pull myself up using the natural steps and craters in the rock wall to balance my feet. The wall was wet, I hoped with fresh water and not salt as I knew I would be thirsty, once I was safe.

My hands were so stiff from the open wounds that it was hard to grip, but I managed to pull myself onto the ledge and lie back on the cold hard stone. I reached over and licked the wall and was eternally grateful that the liquid was both fresh and cool. I was soaked through, but the exertion of running, swimming and climbing had turned it into a wet clammy sweat that would be dangerous later when the night came. I had no choice but to lay here as quietly as I could, listening to the rushing tide, my own racing heartbeat and my growling stomach.

My eye lids grew heavy. I battled with them to stay alert but failed and was awoken by the sound of a boat being pulled on to the sandy opening of the cave entrance and the murmur of gruff low-level voices. I shuddered as there was no sunlight left and the sweat over my body had frozen. Every sound was amplified by the cave walls. If I could hear my blood pumping around my body with fear and my breath rasping, then so could they. The only light in the cave now was the torch light of my Navisian hunters. They moved forward; I could hear footsteps break the sand. I squeezed tight against the wall and was aware of making my breath shallow since everything echoed.

I could not be discovered. Luckily, they had not brought the hounds, so my scent was no longer important. They were so close I could hear their voices.

"How far does this cave go back?" It was a younger soldier's voice, "it's an old pirate hide out - miles I think, there are supposedly tunnels that lead through to the border of Navisian. When trade was not permitted the pirates brought goods in from the sea and then traded in secret."

A deeper, older voice answered, and the flames of torches created shadows along the walls.

"Wow," was the reply, which was quickly interrupted by "stop yacking lads, we need to get this girl and her fairy friend. Lord Railfan demands her and remember she killed Clay." There was real bitterness in that voice, sharp and piercing.

My heart started banging against my ribs I was sure they would be able to hear it.

"What makes you think they are here anyway - they must have drowned surely - they are not natural sea goers remember?" I didn't move one millimetre.

They were now directly below my ledge, so close I could smell their fishy breath and vile sweat.

"We will go deeper, just in case, I'd hate anyone to get away with the murder of one of ours... I don't care about

Lord snooty, I'd rather kill them now than take them back."

There was a hum of agreement and they carried on walking into the depths of the cave. I breathed a sigh of relief but knew this wasn't the end as they would come back this way for their boat and I would still be at risk of discovery. A cramp suddenly caught my calf and I wanted to scream. Not even able to stand for relief, I tried to flex my foot back and forth for some sort of release. It was then that I heard a crack and crumbling sound near my feet and a large piece of my protective ledge fell to the ground. There was a loud crash that echoed through the cave and left my legs exposed up to my knees. I quickly pulled my knees up to my chest and curled into a ball sideways facing the cave wall, my eyes squeezed shut too as I heard the Navisian men rushing back to the crash site.

They looked at the crumbled pile of my ledge and I felt them look directly up at me, I didn't see them as my eyes were tight shut and my breath held in.

"It's just a rock fall." Said one.

"I think we should go - I don't want this to be my tomb and if they are in here the high tide will get them, either that or the lack of food, maybe they'll end up eating each other." They laughed dismissively. I felt sick.

"Ok, let's go." It was the commander's voice again. I heard their footsteps march back toward the opening, but still dare not move; it could be a trick, they may not have gone.

The light from the flaming torches disappeared and I heard the slap of waves on the boat as they pushed off and I breathed.

I sat up, all was dark and the tidal river seemed to be seeping into the cave and up to my safe place. There was nothing I could do I just hoped I would be high enough for the tide not to reach me and that I would survive till morning. And if I didn't make it, well I would be with Brokk, I curled back up and slept.

I was woken by the sun entering the cave, and the first thing I did was reach out for Brokk to tell him we had survived but soon realised he wasn't with me and that empty feeling flooded through me again. I thought I could explore the cave, maybe find some of those tunnels that the soldiers had spoken of - maybe the pirates had left some food? I swung my stiff legs around to jump off the ledge only to find them knee deep in water. The caves were tidal, and I had no idea whether this was full tide or if it was going to rise further.

The water lapped over the ledge and I hugged myself to suppress the shivers that contorted my body. I was at a loss as to what to do, my brain had been on high alert for way too long and I think it was near shut down. 'Should I stand up?' I was worried about doing so as the ledge had already crumbled once. 'Should I swim into the cave with the tide?' I was worried about that idea as I didn't know the strength of the tide or what undercurrents could affect it. I was alone, hunted, trapped. I didn't have the strength to do anything, but I did take my legs out of the water and prayed to the mother of the Oak tree to save me. I reached in my pocket and felt the wet soggy feather and its companion stone from the castle. It was wet but still warm and just knowing it had survived with me gave me comfort.

Something told me to stay put, this ledge had protected me so far and I was going to put my faith in it again. I grabbed on to the jet black, slippery walls behind me and pulled myself up. The water licked my ankles as the base of the ledge was covered. I leant back on to the wall behind me and closed my eyes and envisioned Eveiss and the Meads, going about their business; hunting, eating, laughing, working. In my vision the sun highlighted every blade of grass, every leaf, making it the greenest most beautiful place on earth and the water lapping at my feet became the stream I used for cooling off. My heart was at peace for a moment. I panicked – 'did they know about Brokk?' 'Did they blame me?' 'Did they hate me?' And the beautiful vision disappeared just as the coolness at my feet did.

I shook my head as if to dispel the negative thoughts and opened my eyes, only to realise that the water was retreating, the tide was turning.

Relief is often worse than stress, especially when the body has run on adrenaline for so long and then stops. The total exhaustion that followed was hard to fight against and I knew that my first mission would be to find food to give me the energy to continue. Luckily the tide had brought in a mixture of fish and sea creatures - crabs and shellfish as well as seaweed clumps. I knew these were edible, it's what the Navisians thrived on but it had in turn made me and Brokk sick, as our bodies were not used to it. However, at this point I had no choice, I had to move through the cave whilst there was some light and I needed energy to do it. I picked up a crab and threw it against the rock to break the shell and stun the creature. I then dug out the meat and put it raw into my mouth. I would never be able to make a fire, as any wood close by was wet. The crab tasted salty and the texture was like rubber. I chewed and chewed, finally it broke down enough to swallow. It made me retch but I forced myself to keep it down and I found some black shells and opened them up. I was taking a risk, I had no idea if they were edible but the sticky flesh inside clogged my teeth and tasted like weird metallic meat. I licked the walls to get some moisture inside me and realised that there must be a fresh water source running down into the cave since the river itself, being so close to the sea, must be both fresh and saltwater.

I walked further into the cave, the opening was large so plenty of light flooded in and showed me the way. I hoped the sun wouldn't go down before I found my way out. I was buoyed by the talk of the soldiers about pirates and secret trade routes. If I could only get back to the border and find a tradesman or carter to take me to the battlefields, then I stood a chance of finding my brother.

Walking on the wet sand was hard work, it must have been as hungry as I was as it tried to consume my feet. Looking back, the sea seemed further away than ever. The craggy formations of rock were pretty in the daylight and it reminded me of the Eve Stone mines. However, the Eve Stone mines were much darker, here were more muted shades of brown with green moss deposits and there were strange salt lines made by the tides. Pretty as it was, I felt a sense of urgency as I knew the tide would eventually come to claim the cave for itself once again. I carried on and the deeper I went the darker and duller it became, and my eyes struggled to adjust. I used the harsh stone of the cave wall to guide me, I turned a corner and the final strands of light deserted me. The blackness thrust my imagination into overdrive, probably because of my maddening hunger and heightened anxiety. I thought I was walking on live crab shells and could hear the snorting of a dragon. 'Was this what it was like to go blind and be left with only the inside of yourself, haunted by what you used to see?'

Suddenly a flash of light broke through the curtain of darkness and for a moment I thought it was fire from the dragon's breath, but soon realised there was a small opening in the roof of the cave, just big enough to squeeze a body through. I sighed, half of me as elated as I could be in my exhausted state and half of me defeated. 'How was I going to climb?' I was so fatigued.

I loosened my feet from the sand's grasp and scrambled towards the slither of light. As I got closer, I began to realise just how high up the hole was and I felt deflated. I remembered the times I had climbed up the crumbling walls of Tarnade Castle, and always made it to the top.

'I could do this!'

I took a deep breath and instead of the mouldy darkness of the cave, I felt a cool breeze enter my lungs, as it had when I reached the top of the castle walls and in the freshness of the forest in Eveiss. The breeze brought courage and energy with it, so I braced myself as best I could. As I touched the rough stone to pull myself up, I closed my eyes and imagined the security and sense of home I felt at my castle. I reached up, even further and found a jutting piece of rock and made my first tug towards the light. My leg muscles screeched with effort and disbelief. I winced as the pain travelled through my protesting, broken body as it realised, I would have to do this all again, over and over until I reached the top. I steadied myself and then heaved a breath and reached out, once again grabbing a piece of the greasy rock. It gave way in my hand and cascaded down with the empty thud of defeat. I squeezed my eyes shut and winced.

"Please," I whispered. "Please!" I shouted.

My yell echoed aimlessly around the cave and again I felt completely alone. I rested my head on the cold, wet stone and then without thinking about it, I pushed myself upwards making a grab for the space left by the falling rock. It was a perfect cup shape and my hand fitted nicely. I stabilized my feet and with another exertion of pain, continued upwards without once glancing down at what I had left behind or the path of the fallen rocks. My eyes were fixed to the light. Progress was slow and sore, but finally my hand reached over the rock to the other side of the hole, I felt the crumble of earth beneath my fingers and it was bittersweet. Crumbling earth meant it was unstable but also crumbling earth meant soil, grass and normality.

One last push I told myself.

I could smell *real* fresh air and I desperately wanted to feel it on my face. My scrambling, frantic feet could not find a resting place and I knew in that instant that my tired arm muscles would have to do all the work. I didn't trust that I had the strength. I looked down for the first time since starting to climb and I could see the relentless tide creeping slowly along the floor of the cave below me, wanting to take back possession of it. If I stayed or if I fell, drowning would be the only outcome.

The words of the Mother Willow resonated within me at that moment and I remembered I was an Oak completely; strength and bravery were within me and I was going to draw on them.

Every sinew of muscle protested, "No. No. No!" But my brain was in control so I reached out, let go of my rock stabiliser and for a millisecond hung from one hand, suspended on a precipice, lost between survival and ceasing to exist. The seconds ticked by in my head, as I threw my other arm up and grabbed the other side of the hole, the grass felt wet and my hand slipped - but steadied. I used every last bit of strength to pull myself through the hole and up onto my elbows. My legs hung loose and my arms jerked with shock and exhaustion as I heaved the rest of my body through and landed heavily on my stomach. My cry of anguish was muffled by the wet grassy moss.

I laughed, a relieved, maniacal laugh.

The laugh of someone who felt themselves out of immediate danger but at the same time realised that they were entering a new danger zone.

Exhausted, I just lay enveloped in my grassy pillow.

I don't know how long I lay there, I was in a deep stupor, but from my comfortable mossy pillow, I could hear the rattle of wheels over stones and like an alarm it triggered my brain into alertness. This could be my way out of here, this could be me getting closer to finding Gallam.

CHAPTER EIGHTEEN
THE BATTLEFIELD

I sat up, the blood rushed to my head making my ears echo and my stomach turn over. An old cart was making its way towards me, driven by a figure covered in a thick, tatty sackcloth cloak which framed a face etched in misery. The old horse seemed even older and sadder. As the pair drew nearer, there was no clue as to whether friend or foe. I knew that soon he would pass me by, so I had to take the risk. There was no way I could walk another mile in my weakened state. I stumbled towards the cart flailing my arms feebly.

"Woah!" Ordered the carter forcefully, as he caught sight of me. "Woah there." The old nag was reluctant to stop, doubting that he could get going again. The carter finally came to a halt and I could see a look of shock and apprehension in his eyes. I tried to pull my exhausted self together and look normal.

"Are you going anywhere near the battlefields? Please? I need a lift." I looked up at his gruff face. He grunted, spat and huffed - screwing up his already creased face into a crumpled mess. I doubted he would oblige.

I was astounded when he called me a 'young lady' and suggested I climb up next to him on the driving board.

"Thank you," gratefulness filled my veins and warmed my core.

"No problem, love." He replied and despite his dirty crinkled face and toothless grin, I recognised kindness in him. It had seemed a long time since I had encountered it.

"Lucky you stopped me as I'm taking supplies to the Tarnadian camp, but I'm also hoping to catch sight of my grandsons - their mother does worry - well we all do. What about you?"

"Ah, you're from Tarnade?" It was a bizarre sensation to hear home spoken about.

"Yes, yes, Dove Bridge - you?"

"Yes, near Tarnade Castle. I'm here to find my brother."

"Ah, a sad business this war and you a young girl on her own. It's a long way from home."

I didn't answer, I couldn't.

"You look hungry love, here have some bread, cheese and apple." He handed me a piece of sacking that I opened eagerly and desperately stuffed the stale bread and well-aged cheese into my mouth.

"I can tell you've had hard times - I won't ask." Said my dear rescuer.

"Thank you so much." I mumbled between bites. Finding out this man was a friendly face was a great relief which allowed me to relax and my eyelids drooped.

"You look like you have been through it - why don't you go and lie down in the back, if you're tired? There is fresh straw for the horses and sacks of rice to lay on. Help yourself."

"Thank you again, Sir." I trusted this man, he looked like a murderer, but was as comforting as a nurse. I climbed into the back and the clattering of hooves on the stone path and the distant whooshing of the waves lulled me to sleep.

I was woken by gruff shouting, "Girl, Girl! Battlefield ahead - I will drop you here as I need to make my way to the camp. Good luck to you." He didn't stop the cart but just slowed down slightly. I rubbed the dust out of my eyes, my brain was groggy and my limbs ached like hell. As I jumped off the back of the cart my knees buckled as my muscles clenched. I shouted, "Thank you!" The carter was already off on his way, waving without looking back.

The short encounter of simple kindness was just what I had needed, and I felt refreshed.

I still felt bleary from my sleep, so at first did not see the complete chaos and bloodbath that had taken place before me. No wonder the carter had wanted to get away so quickly. I knew I was in a vulnerable situation; the main battle was obviously over, the corpses were a testament to that, however, there were still skirmishes taking place. I quickly hid behind a large gorse bush jutting up from the baron ground. 'Was I a coward to hide?' 'What else could I do?' I took a deep breath and looked at the devastation before me. I had never seen anything so overwhelmingly distressing in my life, knowing that Gallam could be out there somewhere made it worse. I could have turned away and not looked, but as much as it was horrific and sickening it was also compelling. Something made me study the scenes before me, knowing I would have to physically face them soon enough.

It started to rain, and with it came a cloud of gloom and steam that emanated from the ground. It rained gently at first but then the droplets became slashes and tears that hurt the skin. Smoke from the fires curled through the air like a rope, catching in the back of your throat and making you cough.

In the distance, I could see swords standing as tall as soldiers but on closer inspection, what kept them upright was the sinews of the bodies that they were embedded in. Another corpse was bent double on his knees, with an arrow jutting out of his back, its arrowhead buried deep in his chest. Rat-like, scuttling movements drew my eye to the human scavengers, scurrying over the corpse path and placing reusable weapons into the sacks on their backs. Occasionally they paused and looked with beady eyes and slavering lips at the odd ring or precious jewel that they could recover, by pulling them aggressively off the fingers and necks of the dead.

The field had cleared of fighting soldiers, so I decided to make my foray on to the field, my heart in my stomach, dreading what I might find – 'Gallam, alive or dead?'

It was precarious underfoot, much of the grass was now a mixture of greasy mud and red blood, a slippery quagmire interspersed with severed body parts. The stench made my nostrils flair and my stomach twist and rebel. I retched violently and held on to an abandoned Navisian flag to steady myself. The flag trembled on its pole in the onslaught of rain and the wind teased the torn material open, then closed - so it looked as though it was unsure whether or not it was the victor. In this scene of devastation, I wondered who won was obvious or even important?

Carrion birds swooped and looped over the carcasses. Screeching their own battle cries and laments. In front of me, a single crow landed on the nose of a dead man and tore out his eye. I retched again.

I continued with trepidation, accompanied by the gut-wrenching neigh and shudder of horses as they tried to escape from their riders' dead weights.

I dodged one horse with its saddle hanging half off its flank and the foot of its occupant still caught there.

That strong clawing smell of the abandoned battlefield caught in the back of my throat again, there was so much blood on the field and in the air, I could almost taste the metal. I knew that I had to go on, but I didn't want to, I wasn't sure whether it was the stench or the fear in the pit of my stomach that was making me so sick. All I knew was that I had to search through this uninterred graveyard and perhaps stumble upon my brother. Smoke rose from fires set by the touch of torch to grass, tree or flag cloth, as the victor destroyed everything in its path. The burning added to the seeping silence of the drowned. This was broken only by the odd groan of pain or cry for water. 'Why do those about to die cry for water? Is it cleansing them, or do they hope it will bring them back to life?'

My own lips were parched, not by the sun, but by the heat of oppression that sucked all the moisture from the air. If I'd had water, I would have given it to them but there was no sign of any water anywhere in this forgotten battlefield.

I heard the voices of the Harridans in my head, in Tarnade only they could touch the dead and prepare them for their journey to the afterlife, the place of passing from one form into another: "Never touch the dead for if their eyes meet yours, they will forever haunt you, your eyes are the windows to your soul and it will be your soul that they want and your soul that they will take." I could hear Heligan reciting the old sayings over and over. My mother believed the same, as she would close the eyes of anyone who had passed and would cover their face with a cloth or veil, so no eyes ever met. I shuddered to think of my fate as I prepared myself to come face to face with the dead.

The first dead body I came across was as if he had tried to hold on to life with every muscle of his body, something my brother would have done. Even the cloth of his shirt seemed stiff, probably with dried blood but at this point I couldn't look. My eyes were tight shut and my head turned up to the sky. I was muttering to myself like some madman, "you have to do this...you have to!" I pulled on his shoulder and his weight transferred and seemed to thud onto the ground. It made me let go and start backwards, a reflex forced me to open my eyes and there he was - full of nothingness, like nothing mattered and nothing ever would. Our eyes met but if he had a soul it was long gone and if he had wanted mine there was no longing for it in his eyes.

He didn't look lost or haunted but rightly at peace. There was a mixture of emotions for me; revolt at the injury, certainly pity for the loss of a young life but mostly relief, relief that he wasn't going to steal my soul and relief that it wasn't my brother's eyes staring into eternity.

It was in that moment of relief that I heard a guttural battle cry and looked up to see a mad man running towards me with his sword thrust forward and his eyes burning with hatred for the enemy.

He didn't know me or them or even himself anymore; the stresses of battle had stolen his sanity. I raised my hands to stop him. His war cry burned in my ears and the cold steel of the sword was almost touching me. I realised, in that moment that he wasn't going to stop. I looked down, to see the fallen man had a sword abandoned by his side. I lifted it, surprised by its weight. I wielded it above my head and closed my eyes.

The next thing I knew, I had killed someone else.

It did not shock me. I knew I had changed, I realised what I was capable of, what we are all capable of. I had found an inner strength and fortitude to deal with any situation, I truly was an Oak and Brokk would be proud of me.

I took a deep breath as I effortlessly dropped the sword to my feet and turned on my heel to keep searching for my brother.

CHAPTER NINETEEN
MY BROTHER

I was about to reach down and turn over another body when I felt a hand grip my arm. I gulped back my fear, this was probably the end. The moment suspended in the air along with how far I had come, who I had met and lost, my hopes and dreams for the future.

I sighed acceptance and turned, expecting some blood covered soldier.

I scanned the soldier stood in front of me, slowly identifying the dark hair with the long fringe covering the left eye. I recognised the blue eyes and the hint of a smile through the grime and blood. It was Gallam!

I fell into his arms, a sense of relief overwhelmed me - he wasn't some mangled body on an abandoned battlefield!

"You're alive... you're alive!" I cried into his shoulder.

"Raykal? What are you doing here?" He pushed my shoulders back to have a good look at me, making sure I really was his little sister.

"You look... well... awful," was all he could say, as he ran his eyes over my dirty, weak and mangled body.

"I know, but you look no better Gallam." We laughed, and for a moment we were transported home.

I often had a difficult relationship with my brother, because we were so different in attitude and outlook, but we had an eternal bond that only family brings.

"How's mother?" Of course he thought of her first, he was always her favourite, they had such a close relationship. I realised that hidden inside me all those years was a resentment, I had never recognised or faced before. My journey had opened me up to knowing myself.

"She's been ill, we heard you were missing - presumed dead, it gave her quite a shock."

"That's because I have stopped fighting. War is so chaotic, if you go missing, they presume you've died and that's it. We are holding out in a small encampment in the forest."

I looked closely at Gallam, he still had that air of arrogance he had always carried but it had been softened by understanding. His eyes held a sadness, I wondered if that's what happened to your eyes when life threw its misfortunes at you.

'Did my own eyes, my own windows to my soul, reflect anything of my journey?'

That in turn, made me think about everyone I had known, their eyes showing that inside them they carry a story completely unknown by others.

"We must get out of here Raykal, the war is a mistake! Yes, the Navisian people are ignorant, rude and violent but they keep themselves to themselves. There was no hostility towards us in Tarnade as the Harridans had told us. I have spoken to the common soldiers on the ground and know this to be true. This has been a slaughter with no reason behind it. But since talking to..."

He paused here, as if he didn't want to say the next word. And so, he didn't. He swallowed hard and carried on, "we've been told the Harridans are looking for something, although no one seems to know what, but something important, nonetheless. They obviously thought it might be here in Navisian and that is why the war was started. The Navisian's don't take kindly to interference and invasions into their land. But what angers me most are the lies, all that calling young men to arms over false stories of attacks and rapes. I, and others fell for it and now it all seems so unfair and such a waste."

I could see the disbelief and utter disappointment in his face, how he must have struggled with the fact that his heroes, the Harridans and everything he had fought to become, including earning one of their precious names, had all been for nothing.

"I know they are looking for something Gallam." I was hesitant to tell the full story. Something told me not to at this point. Luckily, he ignored this.

"I have stopped fighting. I and a few likeminded others are hiding out in the woods not far from here. The army encampment is in such disarray they haven't even noticed, or if they have, probably just put us down as missing. We will go there; we will be safer. Follow me."

I did as he said; you did that with Gallam since he had an air of authority. Also, he grabbed my hand and led the way, giving me no choice in the matter. I looked back; the battle area was now being officially cleared by carts from both sides.

I thought I saw my own carter in the mix and hoped that his grandsons were survivors. Gallam pulled me again, with more force.

"Hurry Raykal we don't want to be caught up in this." I smirked, 'back to his bossy ways,' I thought to myself.

We came to a small, hidden encampment which consisted of several other lost souls, war torn, unkempt and dirty. The young men huddled hungrily together around a small fire. They just about managed to raise their heads as I and Gallam approached.

"This is my sister - Raykal." He said. They nodded and moved up to make room around the only piece of warmth and comfort they had. My eyes darted around, uncomfortably; I didn't feel I could say anything. Remembering the horrors of the battlefield - God knows what they had been through and I didn't have any right to break their silence. The atmosphere was heavy with loss, disappointment and a distinct lack of energy.

"We are planning to make our way home, when we can. The war is turning against us, we need to protest to the Harridans to stop this senseless, stupid slaughter."

Gallam spoke directly to me, but the drained men around the fire listlessly nodded their agreement.

"Do you think they will listen Gallam?" From what I had witnessed and learnt I was convinced they would not.

"I'm not certain," he was thoughtful for a moment. "Before I left for the war, I would have said - yes, my faith was with them, but now, knowing what they have done with this war. I'm not so sure."

"I have also learnt a lot about them over the last few months and I don't think they are capable of listening.

You need to be careful, they could imprison you or even worse." I was thinking of Angel, her Skim father and also of Heligan. "They took Heligan you know," I said sadly.

"Did she break the rules?" This sounded like the Gallam from home, the one who always did the right thing and followed what was expected, his short-sightedness made me angry.

"Rules! Gallam, rules! That's all you went on about at home - I'm not interested in rules and now neither are you? You've turned your back on the Tarnade army for a start!" The bitterness in my outburst sparked an interest from our silent companions.

"I don't trust them now," said one young lad of about eighteen with sandy hair decorated with pieces of leaf and mud and dried blood. "Especially after what you told us about your father, Gallam."

"Father?" All I could do was repeat the alien word. "Our father?" I was taken aback to hear a reference to him, we had never really talked about him when we were young. Maybe we had wondered who he was, but we gathered he shouldn't be spoken about in case it upset our mother. There was no hate or malice towards him. We just accepted he wasn't there, and I had not heard anything about him until my mother spoke of him before I left. 'Did she know something more?' She must have realised it was important for me to understand why he left.

"I've met him Raykal and he has stories to tell that will turn your stomach." He looked sheepish, "I'm sorry, I wasn't sure whether to tell you or not."

My mind was working overtime, I too had stories, but then I looked round at the men huddled around the fire and realised that probably we all did. I was not the only one here who was hurt and lonely.

"It's ok," was all I said. I did not know how to feel about my father, but what I could feel rising in my stomach was a mix of resentment and curiosity.

Gallam continued, "I am going to meet him tonight, he is going to help us get home, you must come and meet him." He was unsure of my reaction, he realised I wasn't the same Raykal he was used to.

My reply was stifled to a cry as a man stumbled in through the trees. He flailed one arm to clear the bushes, holding his neck tightly with the other hand. He made sounds like a blocked drain as his neck wound was worsening. His eyes held all the fear that ever existed.

As he reached us a final breath led to him falling face forward on to the fire, extinguishing the small flames of hope. We all sat in shock, not knowing whether to laugh or cry. 'Were we so desensitized now?'

"It took us ages to get that fire going," said a dark scrawny boy, in a monotone voice and lifeless eyes, which answered my question.

Yes, we had become hard and unfeeling.

Another two got up with much effort and moved the body, without looking at him. My brother grabbed me and said, "we'll go and get more firewood." I followed him obediently, but only because I didn't have a choice.
"Are you ok?" He asked, a worried look over his face as he held my arm protectively.

"Yes Gallam, I am not the little sister you left at home. I have seen much worse on my travels. I can cope. I've grown up." I protested.

"I can see that," there was a sadness in his voice, as if he had lost something that he valued. "I suppose you don't need me?" I saw a vulnerability then that I had not really considered with my older brother, but I wasn't ready to deal with it either, I had my own issues to tackle.

"Probably not, but mother does," I deflected, "She needs you and it's important that you get home safely to her. That is why I am here."

"That is my plan Raykal, that's my plan…" He paused, "anyway let's get another fire going and eat before we see father." As he said those words, I realised I was starving.

CHAPTER TWENTY
MY FATHER

It was the first time I had felt really cold, the nip in the air and the bite of the wind told us winter was on its way. Gallam led the way through the battered streets of the small town. It had been hurt by the war, walls were crushed, and fusillades of metal replaced them. Stones and implements of war littered the crooked pathways. The people themselves looked crushed and apathetic, as if they wanted to get over something but didn't have the energy to do so. We twisted and turned for what seemed like an age and finally in some dark backstreet, lit only by a single lantern, we came across an old Inn. Outside was a slumped drunk, hugging his tankard of beer as if it was a golden chalice and mumbling, "it's mine, all mine."

We entered the bar; it didn't smell good, a heady mix of body odour, vomit and over-brewed beer. However, it wasn't raucous, it was quiet and subdued, I supposed because it was early in the evening. Men, many of them soldiers, leant on the bar and others sat at tables playing dice games and drinking.

The only woman I could see was a barmaid, with greasy blond hair and a torn dress, topping up tankards with a jug and winking at soldiers. I felt uncomfortable but Gallam took my arm and led me to a dark corner, where someone in a dark, hooded cloak sat.

The corner was shadowy and the single struggling candle flame from the holder on the table only enhanced this. The hood did its work and prevented anyone from distinguishing features of the person underneath.

"Father, it's me Gallam." Gallam tapped the stranger on the shoulder. The hooded figure looked up and I could see a pair of clear blue eyes. The eyes were enhanced by a pair of ginger brows and the face lit up with a wide toothy grin. I remembered my mother's words as she described my father to me, "he, Regan, was broad and strong with striking red hair and a wide grin that pulled you in and eyes that reflected strength of character, goodness, rebellion and determination to do the right thing."

"Regan?" I asked timidly, "Regan, my father?"

"That's right girl." He stood up to show his broad frame and lifted his hand towards me, "good to meet you at last." I took his hand and the skin felt rough to touch, but it also felt warm and comforting. With his other arm, he reached out to Gallam and pulled us both into a bear hug. It felt wonderful, feeling loved and protected all at once, but I felt that I couldn't give into it so easily. I had to stand my ground. The sullen look I put on my lips was my first barrier. This man had left me, deserted without a backward glance and I wasn't going to let him forget it. We sat down, and Regan took down his hood, so I got to see my father's full face. The chat between Gallam and Regan was flowing and while they talked, I studied his face. He was not attractive in the conventional sense, but his eyes and smile were, as my mother said, what pulled you in.

His eyes were sparkling and lively despite the crow's feet and the deep grey shadows that encased them. They told not only of age but also of agony, hardship and a burden of some sort. The red hair my mother talked of was all but gone, cut short or lost to baldness. His face was open and honest, and I accepted that, despite what he had done, he couldn't be all bad - but I still felt defensive. He turned to speak to me, I didn't hear him at first, I was entrenched in the situation, "Raykal?"

"Raykal?" Then I heard him, but I still wasn't sure if I was ready or wanted to speak to this man.

"Can she speak?" Regan tried to make light of it as he punched Gallam playfully on the arm.

"I can speak."

His face grimaced for a second and I knew it hurt him and part of me wanted it to hurt; to really hurt, the other half of me wanted to say sorry and melt into that bear hug again.

He saw both of these emotions within me and maybe, as a father should, said the right thing. "We do need to speak with each other, to explain, to get to know each other?" What he was saying was true but something in me fought it and I know it reflected in my sullen face. I couldn't forget what I had been through, the friends that I had lost, and I couldn't escape the stupor I was in. Resentment towards this man was rising and boiling over like lava in a volcano and it was as if I was the earth's crust trying to resist the inevitable. My ears filled with a rushing noise and the inane chatter between Gallam and Father became an indecipherable hum. I closed my eyes and instantly regretted it as my lids became a screen on which I saw Heligan being carted away; the contorted face of the brute in his final moments and Brokk's fading body turning to a single feather. Tears tried to wash the pictures away, but I was lost in my own world of being scared, alone and heartbroken. It was then that I felt a hand on my shoulder. It was solid but gentle. I daren't open my eyes, scared that the flood I was holding back would escape, cascade and give away my deep misery; I didn't want my father to see me in a broken state. The hand grabbed my shoulder, more reassuringly, as if they knew. There was only one person it could be... Taliesin. He ruffled my hair as the tears dried and the images faded.

When I finally opened my eyes my father and Taliesin were shaking hands warmly and the sight of his long white hair and tattered cloak were both comforting and soothing to me. Taliesin will know what to do. My brother also shook his hand, and I wondered if they had ever met?

Then he turned and pulled me unceremoniously into his arms and he smelled of mould and rust and trees.

"Taliesin, you smell of home." I whispered.

He patted my back and let me go, looking closely at me as he did so, meeting my eyes and reading my soul.

"Be gentle with this girl, Regan," he said, "She has been through a lot and lost friends along the way. She is older, wiser, maybe tougher but lonelier for it." As usual Taliesin had succinctly summed up everything.

"We have that in common then, my daughter." My father's eyes and mine met and I saw therein so much sadness and loss that I reached out to him and touched his arm. I realised that I did want to get to know this man. I really did.

Also, if I had learned one thing on this journey of mine it was not to judge people too harshly.

"Maybe it's time for you two to have some time alone, while I get better acquainted with Gallam and we work out how to get him and his friends' home." Taliesin pulled Gallam back down into his seat, whilst my father and I went out into the cold air - still touching - I didn't want to let go. The 'slumped' drunk had wandered off somewhere and all was quiet. Only the buzz of muffled voices from the bar broke the peace, a comforting, warm noise that made you feel less alone. The lamps had been lit and their light mixed with the incoming fog created a ghostly feel. We let go of each other in order to wrap our cloaks more tightly around our bodies and smiled at the synchronicity of our movements.

"Let me ask you something Raykal and you don't have to answer straight away," my father began. "Do you have to be with someone to love them or can you be far away, but they are always in your thoughts and you continue to send them all the unconditional love in your heart?" His eyes were serious.

"I think it's important to be there." I was too quick to reply. I wondered if this was my own arrogance talking, wanting to prove I was right, but really thinking about it, 'did I believe this? Had I always loved someone I had never met? Had he loved me even though he was never there for me?'

I was confused. So, confused. But then I thought of Heligan and Brokk, they had gone but I had not stopped loving them. "But yes, I know it's possible to love someone who is not with you." I relented.

"You don't know how important it is to hear you say that, because I have loved you and Gallam and your mother all the time I have been on the road. Do you know why I left?"

"Yes, mother explained before I came on this journey."

"It was not really a choice Raykal, especially the second time; the Harridans made sure of that, but I tried to return. I loved your mother so much, I wanted her to come with me but life on the road for her and children - I don't think it would have been right?" This grown man seemed like a lost little boy at this moment, his soft eyes filling with tears.

"Yes, mother said, she holds no grudges - she still loves you." I saw his face brighten with these words. I couldn't help but love him.

"Those evil hags care for no one other than themselves. Their stupid rules, their abuse of power and their incessant search for immortality has put the lives of miners at risk; has tortured others and they have used their magic to crush people's spirits, turning families against each other." He was bitter now, and I saw the passion that my mother had spoken of in his flashing eyes.

I think I had some of that passion too. I was shocked. 'Did we know the same thing? Did my father know what the Harridans were searching for? Did he know about the Meads and the mine?'

"You know what the Harridans are searching for?" I asked tenuously.

"Yes Raykal, Taliesin has told me that you have spent time with the Meads – I too stayed with the creatures and I too was taken to the mine." I took a sharp intake of breath; the air was cold and it helped to clear my head.

"You lived with the Meads? They said they had another human staying with them, but I had no idea it was you. So, you understand they are not evil? You know their way of life is the right one, how they are at one with nature and…"

He interrupted, "and guardians of the Eve Stone Mine."

"Yes, yes, the Harridans must never discover the mine - I realised its importance - Brokk explained." I felt a shiver as I said his name and my father reached out and touched my cheek in empathy.

"Taliesin explained you had lost some loved ones, I'm guessing this Brokk was one and I'm sorry for it, very sorry." I needed to change the subject before I cried again, but he continued "It was Taliesin who got me out of Tarnade before the Harridans could wreak their punishment. He introduced me to the Meads, who helped me with skills that I would need to survive. Then I travelled on, meeting occasionally with Taliesin, getting updates about your mother, Gallam and you ..." So, Taliesin had known more than he let on, he had never lied though, and it was probably for my own good. I held no animosity to my dear Taliesin.

"Were you given a tree ogham father?" It was the first time I had called him that and I saw the satisfaction on his face. I pulled back my fringe to reveal my tattooed ogham and he instinctively opened his cloak and pulled up his sleeve to reveal his. "Not having much hair, I chose to have mine tattooed on my arm so as not to reveal the Meads' secrets." He explained.

We were both Oaks. We smiled then. However, my father's smile did not last long.

"We can never return to Tarnade - you do realise this? The Harridans use torture and truth drug, they will find out from us where the mine is. It will put the Meads, and indeed all humanity at risk, if the Eve Stone mine is discovered. The Harridans are desperate for immortality so their power and hold over Tarnade can go on forever."

"Never go home? Never?" I remembered that Ammute had already banished me as I hid in the Oak, but I don't think it had really hit me. I always thought that at the end of the quest I would return home to my mother with Gallam, and she would think me a hero. My father realised my shock.

"We are both protectors of the truth and both travellers bound together by what we are privileged to know. However, with privilege comes responsibility." He stared at me with his blue eyes now dripping with kindness.

"I understand." I was genuinely beginning to.

My father continued, "There are lands that you have yet to discover Raykal. Beautiful places and strange smells and even stranger people - adventure and encounters await. I can show you some and we can discover new places together." With these words I was taken back to the Marketplace in Tarnade and the exotic heady herb and spice mixes of Taliesin's potions. Those intoxicating aromas took me to places in my imagination, to think that I could discover them for real with my father by my side! The thought was both amazing and unsettling and my instinct was to reach inside my pocket and touch my trusty stone.

I could feel it's comforting smoothness as well as its natural heat. I realised it embodied a part of the castle that

I loved and part of Eveiss with me everywhere I went. I fought off the homesickness. I brought out the stone so I could hold it in my palm and benefit from its warmth.

My father saw it, "Ah you have a stone that you keep with you?" He asked.

"Yes, I found it at Tarnade castle, it brings me a strange sort of comfort." I opened my palm to show him the stone and he looked at it in amazement.

"I too have a stone I keep with me." He reached inside his pocket and produced a shining green stone, lined with yellow, burnished and glistening as the lamp light caught it. "It's an Eve Stone Raykal - from the Eveiss mine." I think he expected me to be shocked, instead I already knew, thanks to Brokk.

"Yes, I know, it's the same as mine." I looked again at my stone, as if not quite believing that they were the same, but the greenness and lines of yellow confirmed it.

So, we both had Eve Stones with us.

"I got this from the mine when I went there. How did a piece of Eve Stone end up at Tarnade Castle?"

My father twirled his stone in his fingers, "a mystery indeed."

"And something else we have in common."

I couldn't take my eyes off the two stones shining in the lamp light when a single snowflake fell on mine and disappeared instantly because of its warmth. The first snows had started.

"I think we have many things in common Raykal," said my father. "And we will have time to get to know each other properly. We are both banished from our home and we both know the secret that would destroy the world we know, if it should end up in the wrong hands."

As my father said these words, I knew them to be true, we were bound together, not only by blood but by experience. I would have to trust in him, but also trust in myself. I had come through much in a short time and although I mourned my losses, I had grown strong and resourceful. I never belonged in Tarnade.I was my fathers' daughter just as Ammute had said when she banished me.

I looked at my precious stone again, my Eve Stone, with its smooth greenness, mottled yellow fractures and its continuous warmth. This stone wouldn't only represent what I was grateful for but also those precious to me whom I had lost, their energy and spirit and my new-found beliefs and faith.

My father offered me his large, rough skinned hand, with his own Eve Stone in it and I placed my equally rough but smaller hand in his. Our Eve Stones touched, and the heat was instant, our hands were no longer rough but smooth and soft.

We each smiled a knowing smile and we walked hand in hand, through the haze of falling snowflakes back to Gallam and Taliesin, and the rest of our life together.

THE END

NEXT IN THE TARNADE SERIES
THE EVE OF THE OAK

My father and I travelled with Taliesin and Gallam as far as we could; travelling in Taliesin's old caravan, from which he set up at markets and sold his potions. We each took turns to sit up front with him on the driving plank. The alternative was to sit inside.

Here the shelves were full of bottled potions, perfumes, herbs and medicines; they clanked and rattled with every stone or pothole the cart jaunted over. At night there was one pull-out bed, which was basically a wooden plank covered with a sack of straw and an old woollen blanket. The rest of us slept under the cover of the stars or the undercarriage, if it was raining. The warmth of the campfire warmed our bones.

As we got closer to the borders of Tarnade, I could smell home. I struggled with knowing that I could never cross that border. In my memories I could see my mother by the fire, the cat curled contently on her lap. Or maybe she would be making herby poultices and natural painkillers for those she helped as a midwife. What would she do without me? Who would help her after one of her psychic insight; fetch her a cup of water and help her to bed? It would not be me.

Gallam was excited at finally reaching Tarnade after being away for so long, fighting the now condemned war. As we travelled, we passed many returning troops now the war was finally ended. As with most conflicts there were no winners, no gains and nothing achieved. Our little band knew it had all been a distraction by the Harridans so that they could keep on searching for the Eve Stone.

I couldn't get the bloody images of the battlefield out of my mind. The emptiness in the soldiers' eyes as they walked laboriously home, broken and fragmented in mind and body only emphasised the tragedy and waste of it all.

Taliesin was patting Gallam on the shoulder and regaling him with Tarnadian tales, both laughing and nodding furiously. The only one to understand my angst was the man I knew the least in our small party, my Father, Ragan. He took my hand wordlessly, patted it and then kissed it gently. All the time looking earnestly into my eyes. I couldn't return his honest gaze.

We hadn't been able to go the quickest way home. To pass through Eveiss where The Meads lived would have been unsafe, as we could put the Eve Stone Mine in danger. Also, I had a personal reason not to want to face The Meads, whom I loved and respected deeply, knowing that I had let one of their own die. I had failed to protect Brokk and keep him safe even after being asked and trusted to do so. There was no way I could face them. And so we had left Navisian and followed the water to Rivers Forge and into Elmet, with its open moors of grazing sheep and oases of apple orchards. We planned to part at Derva Forest on the border.

Derva Forest was a difficult place, it was known for being impenetrable and was left to the rule of nature and wildlife. This made it safer for my father and myself as we were less likely to meet anyone and the fewer people we met the less likely we were to have to explain ourselves.

The goodbyes were short and difficult. Gallam knew I was giving up the chance to go home but really didn't understand why. Our father, a strong and burly man, was tearful and full of emotion, which Gallam found difficult to cope with. Taliesin stood back awkwardly, an outsider to this family farewell. We hugged and shook hands bravely. My father put a letter into Gallam's hand for our mother and I told him to tell her I loved her.

The caravan pulled away, with a final wave of a hand. I swallowed hard, dowsing my emotions. Would I ever see Gallam or Taliesin again? Or my home?

As the last clinks and rattles of the caravan disappeared my father and I, lone travellers for the first time, entered the forest. He had the hood of his cloak pulled over his head, hiding his grief and I followed suit with my head bowed down to the forest floor. We walked in silence for a while both struggling with our feelings of loss. My father broke the silence.

"We should stay within the forest for a while Raykal. I came here when I first left Tarnade, it made me feel close to my family, without actually being able to be with them… it is relatively safe and rare that humans venture in so it will give us time to plan."

I nodded hopelessly. What did I know about being a wanderer?

The forest was thicker than I had encountered, even in Eveiss. The floor was matted with vegetation, a carpet of mushed leaves, so many had fallen it seemed the forest was in a constant autumnal state. Moss and ferns worked as a team to claim everything as their own. Not one tree grew straight, but all were twisted and anchored into each other, their roots mangled into shapes, like the clawed feet of mythical dragons. Slippery slate intermingled with wet rocks making walking treacherous and overhead were stones jutting out from crags that looked like the heads of angry snorting bulls. It was permanently dusk here; the canopy of trees was so thick and protective that little sunlight battled its way through. This terminal twilight added to the mystery and disorientating nature of the place. Nothing was recognisable, everything looked strange. There was no bird song, just rustles in the bushes to signify movement of woodland creatures, probably watching us with curiosity.

As we struggled to walk without tripping or sliding, we were hampered even more by misty swirls that encased us in their smoggy gas; then disappeared as quickly as they had arrived. This forest world was disorientating and disturbing.

We came across a stream with a soft, moss-covered bank that was clear of roots and stones, so we decided to settle there for the night. I collected as much dry wood as I could carry to build a fire, whilst my father picked a selection of the copious mushrooms from this moist dark haven. His backpack was a glorious holdall of many useful things, including an essential knife and cooking pot. As the flames licked the pot, another heavy mist descended. Seeing the worried look on my face, my father reassured me.

"Just sit it out Raykal, it will soon pass." He continued to calmly stir the mushrooms in the pot and the smell was earthy and delicious.

The mist became broken and wispy like frozen breath and I was able to see around me again. Placed within the stream was a small island with a large birch tree on it, its once white trunk was claimed by the moss, as was everything in this place. There was a piece of broken trunk protruding out from the base, it was an unusual shape almost like a human on his knees, head bent down to pray. Everything in this place could be something else, there were so many green moss-covered warped shapes. This one, however, made me do a double take. It was moving! The shape was elongating as if it was standing up!

"Ragan!" I called my father tentatively, unsure of what I had seen. Then more panic-stricken, "Father – look!"

The shape was now standing tall, it had its back to us and was facing the tree, I could see a cloak of green moss but also the definite legs of a man. My father looked up just as the green man turned and jumped effortlessly from the small island and on to our bank. I instinctively reached for my knife in my boot - ready to strike but my father pulled my arm down gently.

"Steady Raykal - this is not an attacker."

I looked curiously at him, but he didn't take his eyes off the green stranger standing before us. I saw a glint of recognition and then he stood up and was shaking the green man's hand enthusiastically. The man before us was covered from head to calf with a green moss cloak only his weathered face and his feet were visible traces that he was human. His dirty face was caked in mud as were his hands; as he reached out to shake mine. I was unsure, but my father's knowing smile reassured me.

"Don't worry Raykal, we have met before... this is Beyon and he is a member of The Guardian of The Birch..."

COMING SOON

ACKNOWLEDGEMENTS

This book is steeped in nature and the environment and I would like to acknowledge all those that fight for animals and saving the planet - there is nothing more important. We must keep fighting animals do not have a voice and the earth is dying.

For the underlying spirituality and magic within the novel I would like to thank my husband Andy. He took me on journeys, where we discovered not only beautiful places, but also ancient spiritualism – The Celts, ogham's, the magic of nature and, of course, Merlin. All these adventures and stories inspired me greatly and I couldn't have done it without him.

I would also like to thank many of the students that I tutored at St Christopher's School, Letchworth. As a tutor you get to know your students well and they encouraged me to keep on writing when I felt like giving up. Thank you so much for your enthusiasm, advise and encouragement.

A big thank you to all the authors out there who have inspired me to want to write myself. Since I was a child, I have loved reading and have appreciated the escape to other worlds, places and times your books have taken me to. You all allowed my imagination to soar.

Finally, books cannot be written without support and I would like to thank all my family and friends for putting up with me.

ABOUT THE AUTHOR

Jayne would describe herself as a free thinking, creative, socialist, nature loving weirdo. She is passionate about the environment, history and reading. She has written stories and poetry all her life but this is her first novel. She has three grown-up, independent and usually totally embarrassed children, three lovable cats who are completely bonkers, three beautiful albeit crazy hens and she lives with her relatively normal husband Andy in Bedfordshire.

BV - #0033 - 270220 - C0 - 198/129/12 - PB - 9781916225145